A Cowboy for Merry

A Cowboy for Merry

A Three Sisters Ranch Romance

Jamie K. Schmidt

TULE
PUBLISHING

Chapter One

MERRY GRAYSON LOVED Baradero, Argentina. The countryside, the colors, the food, and the hot gauchos who flirted with their eyes made her feel that she could do anything.

The small hospital the paramedics insisted she go to—not so much.

"I'm fine," she said, then tried to say it in broken Spanish when the nurse didn't respond to her. "*Yo estoy bien.*" Merry's Spanish wasn't very good. It had been a long time since Senora Martinez's high school class kept her on her toes. *Mas tequila*; *Donde esta el bano?* and a handful of colorful swear words were her entire repertoire.

"You are not fine. You have a concussion, and we're still waiting for X-rays on your ribs and shoulders," the nurse said in flawless English.

Merry rotated her shoulder. It did hurt. So did her ribs, but she knew they were just bruised instead of cracked. She'd had cracked ribs before and remembered the pain keenly.

"I don't need to wait here for the results, right?" Her bed in the Howard Johnson's downtown was calling her, along with a shot of whiskey for the pain.

The nurse frowned. "Do you have anyone to look in on you?"

The question hurt almost as much as her shoulder. "No," Merry said softly. Her sister June had decided to stay stateside to be closer to her new boyfriend, Esteban, instead of competing in Argentina this year. Her friends, Carly and Zane, who she had been supposed to spend her birthday and Christmas with had stayed for the rodeo, but then had flown off without her when it looked like she wouldn't be able to join them. Even her horse, Raphael, hadn't made the trip to South America with her. He probably was being spoiled rotten by her best friend, Janice Sullivan, at the Three Sisters Ranch in Last Stand, Texas.

Merry was in Argentina to compete in the new bronc-busting event that the Women's Professional Rodeo Circuit had just introduced. She wasn't very good at it yet, and these international events were one way to get practice in without affecting her ranking.

"The IWPRC requires that you stay here overnight, then."

"Great," Merry said, forcing a small smile. She didn't want to give the nurse a hard time.

The International Women's Professional Rodeo Circuit wasn't taking any chances for lawsuits, not that Merry would sue them anyway. One Grayson sister in litigation at a time was enough for their family. Right now, June had dibs on that because of the way the IWPRC's U.S. counterpart had handled a public relations nightmare between June and her rival, Shayna James.

"Can I at least get dressed?" Merry hated the thin hospital gown and the bed was equally uncomfortable.

"I'm sorry," the nurse said, and actually looked like she meant it. "Would you like some juice?"

Not without vodka. "Just some water, thanks."

The nurse gave her a sympathetic smile and left.

Merry shared her hospital room with two other women. She could hear them moving around, but the thick curtains gave them all a semblance of privacy. Luckily, she still had full bars on her phone. Unluckily, her mother had already called twice.

Groaning, Merry sunk her head back onto the lumpy pillow. She knew what her mother was after. The rodeo hadn't been televised, and Penny Grayson didn't do the internet. So she had no idea that Merry had been thrown ass over teakettle and nearly stomped to death by a bronc. The damned horse had had it in for her, too. If she'd wanted that type of danger, she would have taken up bull riding. At least they had bullfighters—rodeo clowns—to protect the riders after they got thrown.

No, her mother was blowing up her phone because she wanted Merry to come home to Last Stand for her birthday, which was on Christmas Eve, and then stay for Christmas and New Year's. Normally, that wouldn't be a problem. But she had been home only a few months ago for Emily Sullivan's wedding. And while it had been great to see her family and her old friends, it had also been...not so great.

Her sisters June and April seemed to be settling down in Last Stand, mostly due to their connection with the Sullivan family and their Three Sisters Ranch. Merry had known the Sullivan sisters all her life. They were the same age as she and the rest of her sisters, although they had lost touch for a few years. Around the holidays, they would circle back into each other's orbits, and it was like no time had passed between them.

It would be nice to spend time with her family again, but Merry was acutely aware that her sisters had leveled up without her. Sure, Merry had won multiple women's rodeo championships and taken home hefty purses and diamond-studded belt buckles, but her sisters were actually happy and content with their lives. When the hell was that going to happen to her?

It had been a long time since she felt any sense of peace—just the grim satisfaction of a job well done. She was damn proud of her achievements—even if she had lost to her baby sister in the final round of barrel racing last season. Merry didn't begrudge June the win. June had deserved it after the shitty year she'd had, being blacklisted by the WPRC because of a bullshit smear campaign.

Truth be told, Merry wanted to move on from the rodeo. She had done all she could and, after fifteen years of being on the road, she was ready to give her horse and herself a rest. She should have done it last year when she had a sweet job lined up announcing at the various rodeos with the broadcast team. A part of her wondered, though, if that would get boring too after a while. Restlessness seemed to be a family trait. But Merry wanted to retire from the rodeo on her own terms. And that meant winning the buckle and a fat purse for WPRC's first women's bronc-busting event.

Maybe it was the Christmas season in general that had Merry all melancholy and retrospective. When she'd been growing up, Christmastime had been magical. She was named Merry, after all. Her mother always made sure that her birthday on December twenty-fourth didn't get lost in the shuffle. Her father, Luke, would always show up too, usually dressed like Santa and bearing presents for her, as well as for her sisters, April and June.

But as they all got older and life's responsibilities had gotten in the way, Christmas and her birthday had become less magical. As Merry had gotten famous, or infamous in the rodeo circuit, there were a lot of rich fans who loved to be able to fly her all over the country, and she'd lived it up, enjoying the good life for a few years. The mile high club was a good time, and partying in a private plane pretty much ruined her for commercial air travel.

This year was supposed to have been epic. Carly and Zane were going to fly her to Tahiti, where she could spend her birthday with her butt in the sand and Christmas drinking rum, surrounded by men in tight bathing suits. If that wasn't the perfect birthday Christmas combo, nothing was. Unfortunately, they took off without her, leaving her wondering about her next step.

Her phone rang again and Merry answered it right away so it didn't disturb the other patients in her room. "Yeah?" she said in a low, quiet voice.

"Finally," her mother screeched.

Wincing, Merry pulled the phone away and lowered the

volume. Her head was throbbing now in time with her ribs. Penny Grayson was not a quiet woman.

"What's up?" Merry asked, settling into a reclining chair by the window. She hissed in pain. It felt like she had been skewered like a kebob.

"What's wrong?" her mother asked.

"Bad connection. I'm tired. Can we talk tomorrow?" Merry eased her feet up and tried not to whimper. She should have taken the acetaminophen instead of toughing it out. When the nurse came back with the water, she would ask for some.

"I'll let you rest as soon as you tell me when you're landing."

"I didn't fly out with Carly and Zane," she said. "They had places to be that I wasn't interested in going." A big fat lie. She hadn't been allowed to fly out with them, unless she wanted to breach her IWPRC contract—she had to be cleared by the hospital before she went anywhere. And they hadn't wanted to wait around.

"When are you coming home, then?"

"I don't know. I don't have my schedule handy." Merry closed her eyes. It hurt to think.

"Well, I do. You don't have an event until the new season starts in February."

"That long?" Merry frowned and then immediately regretted it as pain lanced through her skull.

"You could use a vacation."

Couldn't argue with that. But she had been leaning more toward Tahiti than Last Stand.

"And we'd like you home for your birthday and Christmas."

"Why?" Merry complained. "They're just regular days."

"No, they're not," her mother shouted and a blast of white-hot pain flashed through Merry's entire being.

"Please, don't yell," she growled.

"Then don't talk nonsense."

Merry tried not to engage, but it wasn't in her nature to let things go. "We're all adults. Newsflash, Ma, there ain't no Santa Claus and even if there was, I'd be on the naughty list."

Her mother snorted. "You and me both."

Merry couldn't remember if her mother was still seeing the owner of the trailer park that she rented her plot from or if she had moved on. Her mother tended to go through boyfriends like Merry rode around barrels.

"I want all of us together this year."

"Has Luke called?" Merry wondered if her father was in the neighborhood. He traveled all over, plying his trade as a mechanic, too restless to stay in one shop for any length of time. If her father was in Texas, maybe they could have an old-fashioned Christmas like they used to have. It wouldn't be Tahiti, but it wouldn't be a totally depressing suckfest either.

"No, but we don't need him."

"You don't need me," Merry said, thinking that her two sisters and their boyfriends would take up more than enough space in the double-wide for Christmas dinner.

"Of course, I need you. You're my daughter. It won't be

the same without you." The little wobble in her mother's voice hurt worse than her head. Besides, what was Merry going to do until February anyway?

She wasn't about to chase Carly and Zane around the world, even if she could afford to do it. Argentina would be a nice place to hang out over the holidays, but she couldn't imagine anything more depressing than a solo dinner at HoJo's on her birthday and Christmas.

"Raphael is probably wondering if you've abandoned him," her mother said casually.

Ooh, now she was fighting dirty.

"My horse is being well taken care of, as I'm sure June has told you." Between Janice Sullivan and Merry's sister June, Raphael was being spoiled rotten.

"It's not the same, though, is it?" her mother said with mock sympathy.

It wasn't. She missed her horse. And if she was being honest, she did miss her family and her real friends. Merry was pretty sure Janice Sullivan wouldn't have flown off and left her in a hospital all alone in a foreign country. And when she was with Carly and Zane, she always felt that she had to be Merry Grayson, one of the wild Grayson sisters. It was exhausting to always have to be "on."

She sure as hell found out this Christmas the people she was partying with weren't really her friends. Still, it was hard not to feel dejected at the thought of spending Christmas back in Last Stand. But maybe it would do some good for her to go home and think about her life and her next steps in her career. She was used to being on top at the WPRC. Now her rankings would slip because of that stupid bronc-busting category. She felt so conflicted about her life. While Merry wanted to be the first woman to win the buckle in that category before she retired, she and Raphael should have retired last year.

"What do you want for your birthday and Christmas?" her mother asked, probably to fill up the long silence.

"New pair of boots," Merry said. Although, a sexy cowboy looking for a good time, a couple of shots of Fireball Whisky and a long rest in a comfortable bed, also came to mind.

To retire or not to retire? That was the question. If she could win in a category that had never been offered before, Merry's name would forever be etched in the WPRC history. But she would have to beat younger, more talented riders who had trained longer. Still, she knew that if she retired now without having won the distinction, people would eventually forget about her. And if they did, who was she without the rodeo? Merry didn't know, and that scared her. She wanted to be remembered as a hell of an athlete and a force to be reckoned with.

That was what she really wanted for Christmas.

The nurse came back with a pitcher of ice water. Merry held her hand over the receiver and whispered, "Can I get some Tylenol?"

The nurse placed a little plastic cup with two pills by the water. "I thought you might change your mind."

"You're the best. Thanks."

"What's going on?" her mother asked again.

"Nothing," Merry said. "Took a knock in the arena today. It's not a big deal."

"Are you sure?"

"Yeah." She hoped she sounded convincing.

"Do you want to talk about it?"

"Not one little bit," Merry said, even though she knew it would entice her mother. "I'll tell you when I see you."

That sidetracked her. "When?"

"I'll look into getting a flight out as soon as I wind up my business here," Merry said.

"This is going to be the best Christmas ever," her mother said, hanging up.

Merry wasn't too sure about that, but it wasn't going to be the worst. Not by a long shot. That one was reserved for the time she and her boyfriend got shot at.

Simon Reynolds had been her first love, and in a lot of ways, her only love. He had been her shoulder to cry on when her mother had finally gotten around to divorcing Luke, even though their marriage had been over for years.

With Simon, Merry could be herself instead of what Luke and her mother expected her to be. Simon hadn't cared about her grades, or her standings in the teen rodeo. He was fun personified and she had loved him deeply. Then he got sent to prison for a bunch of things she had been too naïve to have known about, and she had never heard from him again. He probably hated her for not speaking up at his trial or fessing up that she had been with him the night he was arrested. The old guilt still felt fresh, and she forced thoughts about Simon aside.

"Guess I'm going home for Christmas," she said with a sigh. Visions of palm trees and fruity drinks danced in her head before being replaced by a dusty trailer park and a bucket of ice filled with White Claw. It wouldn't be Tahiti, but it would be home.

Chapter Two

SIMON REYNOLDS WAS surprised to find a car and driver waiting for him when he stepped through the gated, electric fence of Beaumont Federal Correction Institute.

"See you around, Reynolds," the guard said with a smirk.

"Don't bet on that," Simon said. He was never coming back here again. He was no longer the dumb kid with a chip on his shoulder with a burning desire to shame his father into oblivion.

Even if his father hadn't just died, Simon wouldn't be boosting cars for a living anymore. He had done his time, learned his lesson, and was ready to move on with his life. Move on to what, though? That was still up in the air. But for the moment, it was enough that he was no longer in prison.

The driver straightened up from where he had been leaning on the spotless Lincoln Continental. "I'm Charlie Lincoln," he said. "We spoke on the phone."

Charlie was a distinguished-looking man with white hair and sharp green eyes. He dressed like a businessman instead of a social worker. Simon felt a little shabby in comparison, but he shook his outstretched hand anyway. "Yeah, but I thought my parole officer said the outreach program doesn't start until Monday." As a term of his early release, Simon had to work on a cattle ranch for a month to reintegrate himself into society. It sounded like free labor for the ranch owner to Simon, but it had shaved six months off his sentence, so it was worth it.

"It does, but I saw that you had scheduled a ride service through our office to come pick you up. I figured I'd save you some money and introduce myself at the same time."

"It's a four-and-a-half-hour ride."

"I had some time to kill."

Simon was blown away by the kindness. "I appreciate that." Simon tossed his backpack into the back seat and climbed into the passenger's side. He hoped that Charlie wasn't a Bible thumper or an MLM salesman in his spare time. "I can help you out with gas money, if you need it."

"I write it off on my taxes. Besides, it gives us a chance to get to know each other."

There was the catch. Still, Simon was grateful for the ride and figured he could deal with whatever Charlie was selling.

"Where can I take you?" Charlie asked.

"My mother's house. I guess it's my house now." His father had left him everything, but there was no way in hell he was going there. Too many bad memories. It still blew his mind that after all the bad blood between them, Braxton Reynolds had kept him in the will. Simon rattled off the address to his mother's place. It was a cabin really. It probably needed a shit ton of work after being neglected for almost eight years. But it was still better than going anywhere his father had lived.

"My sympathies. How did your father pass?"

"Alone," Simon said. It seemed like Charlie was a talker, not a salesman. That didn't seem so bad. Except the last thing Simon wanted to do was talk about his father.

He hadn't seen or spoken to him in ten years. Mostly because his father had used all his influence to put Simon behind bars in the first place. Not that Simon hadn't deserved it, but he had only been a dumb kid. Simon forcibly pushed the memories aside before the familiar acid of betrayal choked him.

"I'm sorry."

"Don't be. He brought it on himself." Braxton had been a womanizer with a mean temper and held grudges that dated back to his playground days. He might have softened a bit in his old age, but it had been too late for the two of them. Maybe if his mother had lived, instead of drinking herself to death, they might have had a shot at reconciliation. But she died while Simon was in prison, and at that point, he decided he was an orphan.

Simon had even refused to see him when his father had tried to visit him in prison. And Simon had ripped up all his father's letters unread. He didn't need to be berated long distance while he was behind bars. If the old man had wanted redemption in his final days for being a colossal prick his entire life, Simon didn't have the power or the desire to grant him absolution. The only letter Simon hadn't thrown away was the one that was with the packet of paperwork that the lawyer had given him about the inheritance.

He wasn't sure why he hadn't chucked it like he had the previous ones. Maybe because it was the last letter his father would ever send to him. That didn't mean he wanted to read what the man had to say. Especially, since he wouldn't be able to argue or rail at a dead man. Someday, he might read it. Or he might toss it in the fire and let it burn.

For a rich man, Braxton had very little of it left by the time he died, but there was enough to keep Simon afloat for the rest of his life. But fuck that. He didn't want a damned thing from the old bastard. His mother had left him a very small inheritance too, as well as the run-down cabin. He would live off that while he tried to get his life back on track.

Thanks, Mom, he thought as he looked down at his hands. He wished he could have told her that in person. As well as apologize for giving her gray hairs when he was a teenager.

Eloisa St. Clair had been Texas oil royalty. Braxton had married her for her social contacts as well as her wealth. She was old money, and he was new money. Together they had been going to build a dynasty. Except Braxton couldn't keep it in his pants, and his grandfather had disowned his mother when she married Braxton.

He was going to sell his father's house and his car at the first opportunity and donate the money to charity.

Well, maybe not the car.

It was a purple ZR-1 Corvette. The old man got it fresh off the line in 2009. At the time, it was the fastest Corvette ever built—the first supercharged 6.2-liter V8 engine in Corvette history; 638-horsepower. It went from zero to sixty in three and a half seconds. The top speed was two hundred and five miles per hour. When Simon pinned the accelerator to the floor, it had felt like flying. It also made Merry Grayson agree to go out with him. The grin on his face felt strange. He wondered if it still ran well or if his father had fucked that up too.

"Are you doing all right?" Charlie asked. "I know being out can be a big adjustment."

"So far so good." Truth be told, he hadn't thought about it until Charlie mentioned it, and now a slight trickle of anxiety coated the back of his throat.

"I was in for twenty years. Fraud."

"GTA," Simon said. "But I guess you know that from my file. What made you go into this line of work?"

"I got my master's in social work inside and thought it would be a good place to start as any. Helping out ex-cons like me. Maybe I'm trying to make amends as well as make a living. Do you smoke?" Charlie reached inside his jacket pocket for a pack of cigarettes.

Simon almost took one. He didn't smoke, but a cigarette could be useful inside. Except, he wasn't inside anymore. And if he wanted a candy bar or a magazine, he'd buy one instead of trading for it. "Nah, I'm good. I got my bachelor's degree inside. Liberal arts, mostly because I wasn't sure what I wanted to do. Still don't."

"You'll figure it out. Do you mind if I light up? I'm trying to quit, but it's an addiction."

"Go ahead." The smell didn't bother him. In fact, it was comforting in an odd way. There was too much sky outside and too much scenery rushing by. It put him on edge. He resisted the urge to look behind him as phantom fingers ghosted over his neck.

"Are you planning on continuing to work on a ranch after the integration session?" Charlie lit up and took a deep pull. He cracked the window and blew the smoke out of the car.

That's what Simon had put on his application because he thought it would give him a better chance of being accepted into the program. "Maybe." It was as good of a place to start as any. He had no fucking idea what he wanted to do with the rest of his life—aside from the fact he was done stealing cars. "Is the ranch that we're working at hiring?"

"Not at the moment, but I could ask around for you."

"Thanks."

"You got a girl waiting for you?" Charlie asked.

Simon's mind flashed on Merry Grayson again. He had made sure that she didn't wait around for him ten years ago. But man, he'd love to see her again. It was hard to follow women's rodeo in Beaumont, but he'd get snippets of information when he could.

"There's no one," Simon said. "Not anymore."

He wondered what Merry was doing now. Every now and then he'd catch a glimpse of her on ESPN or come across a newspaper or magazine article with her in it. He had a half-assed scrapbook of what he had collected over the years. It had got him into a couple of fights, but it had been worth it. Not being in a cell or in a prison yard with fifty other men was going to take a lot to get used to.

"You a football fan?" Charlie asked, fiddling with the radio until the Cowboys's game came on.

"I can take it or leave it. I like rodeo."

"Then you're going to like the Three Sisters Ranch. Trent Campbell, the bull rider, has a school on the property. And June Grayson, the barrel racer, hangs around all the time because her boyfriend is the assistant foreman. You'll be working with Esteban during the session. He's a good guy. You play poker?"

"Some." Simon's body went on full alert at Merry's sister's name.

"Well, don't. The boys get together for a Friday night poker game. I don't want to write you up for a parole violation."

"I'm not going to risk that. Not for poker anyway." He gave Charlie a quick grin to show that he wasn't serious. Simon wondered how to ease into the question he really wanted to ask, but then just decided to come right out and say it. "Does Merry Grayson ever come around?"

"I've only seen her at the ranch for my son's wedding. The Grayson sisters are close to the Sullivan sisters. My son, Donovan, married Emily Sullivan."

"So, you're part of the family."

Simon caught a flash of something in Charlie's expression before he masked it with an indifferent shrug. "Something like that. It's complicated."

Since Simon knew all about complicated, he didn't press the issue. He wondered if Charlie had any wedding pictures with Merry in them on his phone. There wasn't any way he was going to ask, though.

The drone of the football game and the comfort of the seat made it easy to nod off. After the second time he jerked his head up from a light doze, Charlie chuckled. "Ease the seat back and get some rest."

"I don't mean to be bad company."

"You're safe. Rest easy. You're going to need it in the upcoming weeks."

Simon appreciated the thought and was out almost as soon as his noggin hit the lowered headrest. He woke up a few hours later when Charlie stopped to gas up.

"I'm going to stretch my legs," Simon said, groaning and stretching as he got out of the car.

"Take the opportunity to use the can too. I'd like to drive straight on to Last Stand," Charlie added.

Nodding, Simon headed into the little convenience store attached to the gas station. He stopped, dazed at all the choices. He pulled out his wallet and checked that he had enough money for a soda and a candy bar. He only had twenty bucks, but the ATM card that had been in the paperwork would access the bank account that his father's attorney had set up for Simon. He was damned if he was going to use it if he didn't have to, though. Simon didn't need anything from that bastard. He'd use the money from his mother's estate to get a few things later. Poking his head out the door, he called out to Charlie. "You want anything?"

"Large coffee, black, and a doughnut."

"You got it."

He asked for the restroom key first from the clerk behind

the counter. When he closed the door behind him, he marveled that the restroom was bigger than his cell. After taking care of business, he washed up, splashing cold water on his face. The man staring back at him in the mirror looked scared.

"It's real," he said, startling a little at how loud his voice sounded. "It's real." It had been five years since he had any freedom at all. And back then, he'd only had it for a month or so before he had fucked up and stolen another car. Then he'd gone right back inside.

"Not this time," he told the man in the mirror.

After tossing his paper towel into the trash, Simon went back into the store to gather up road trip snacks. Another memory of Merry flitted through his mind. When they would go driving, she would bring a bag of beef jerky and strawberry licorice to share. He picked those up along with a Coke for him and Charlie's order. Telling himself not to spend the whole twenty dollars before he could access his mother's estate account, he plunked his purchases on the counter.

And there she was.

Merry was grinning back at him from the cover of *Cowgirl Today* magazine. Simon didn't care that buying the magazine brought him down to his last dime. It was worth it. She was beautiful. And happy, which was all he ever wanted for her.

"You got everything?" Charlie asked when he got back to the car.

"I'm all set." He would need to get the banking stuff in

order soon, so he was only using his mother's money and not his father's. There was so much shit to do and things to think about...like who the hell was going to hire an ex-con in a job that he could afford to live on. But he gave himself permission not to think about it until later. For now, all he wanted to do was chew on a Twizzler and read the article about his first love.

Chapter Three

M ERRY GRAYSON HAD mixed feelings about being back in Last Stand, Texas. It was damn cold for Texas, even if it was December. But that might be because she was used to the sultry Argentinian nights. She was currently shoulders-deep in a large hot tub on the back porch at Janice Sullivan's retreat center at the Three Sisters Ranch. Janice was on the other end of the tub rocking a red bandana-patterned bikini and she had cucumber slices over her eyes.

Merry was wearing a Texas flag one-piece bathing suit that one of her sponsors had given her. She hunkered down into the hot water and let the strong pulsating jets pound into the sore muscles of her shoulder and back. She probably had been in the tub too long, but she was willing to risk looking like a prune to have the warmth soothe all her various aches and pains. She was still sore from being thrown by the bronco she had been trying to ride in the international rodeo.

She had gotten lucky though. After falling, she had dodged the horse's back hooves, and missed being kicked in the face by inches. Ever since, she'd had nightmares about picking up her teeth as if they were spilled Chiclets on the ground.

Merry wasn't in a big hurry to get back into the saddle, but the hundred-thousand-dollar purse for first place in the new bronc-busting category was calling to her. The reason the winner received so much money was to entice women into entering the new category for the new season. There hadn't been a lot of takers before they upped the prize money to six figures. It was a rough and brutal event. But money talked.

And one hundred large ones would be a nice retirement package for her. It would allow her to pay off her credit cards and get an apartment somewhere nice.

But first, Merry needed to practice, if she wanted any chance at winning. And even then, it might not be enough. Once the WPRC upped the prize money, the competition became fierce, but there was only one rider who was outriding all of them: LeAnn "Killer" Keller. Eighteen years old and full of piss and vinegar. She reminded Merry a lot of herself when she'd first started. LeAnn was the one to beat.

"I got a favor to ask you," Janice said.

"I knew there had to be a catch to this hot tub invite." Merry propped open one eye and stared at her friend.

The Three Sisters Ranch had originally been just a cattle ranch and farm, but when hard times hit, Janice and her two sisters had put the ranch's acres to good use by expanding into other areas.

Janice, who was married to the ranch's foreman, Nate, had opened up a retreat center where her clients got to enjoy life as a cowboy or cowgirl for a few days. Merry and Janice had the retreat's hot tub to themselves for the time being, but Merry knew Janice had a full schedule of guests this week.

"I can see that you're a little beat up from that last rodeo," Janice said. "But can you manage to get back on a horse in a couple of weeks for a charity event?"

"As long as it's not bronc riding—or bull riding." Another one of the ranch's new businesses was a bull-riding school that former championship bull rider Trent Campbell had opened. Janice's sister Kelly had married him a few years ago. Kelly had a portrait studio on the ranch and supplemented her business by taking pictures of her husband's students and class pictures.

"No, nothing like that," Janice said, waving her hand. "I was thinking barrel racing."

That was much better. Her horse, Raphael, would like the exercise and the chance to show off to cheering fans. "What's the charity?" Merry asked.

"The families of Last Stand have been hit pretty hard by the pandemic. Trent's having a Christmas event at the rodeo school. We were hoping having a big name like you could draw in some out-of-towners and we could sell tickets. The money would go back into the community just in time for the holidays. It would really help some of the struggling families."

Since Merry had been one of those struggling families growing up, she was completely on board. "Sure. What can I do to help?"

Janice sat up so quickly, the cucumbers plopped into the

water. She tossed them out into the scrub brush off the porch. "Everyone is looking at a rematch between you and June."

Merry chuckled. "Not to mention that Emily probably wants in on the action too."

Emily was the youngest Sullivan sister. She ran the cattle ranch, which was a trip because she was a dedicated vegetarian. Her husband also had a business on the Three Sisters Ranch. Donovan offered nature safari tours for tourists, and did hunting excursions when the feral hog problem got out of hand.

Janice snorted. "Like she's got a chance in hell against the two of you."

Shrugging, Merry said, "It depends on the horse, the rider, and the time of day. Do you want me to talk to June about this?" She knew just where to look for her sister—sneaking smooches with Nate's second-in-command behind the barn. Esteban was okay in her book. He had supported June when the WPRC had played her dirty and blackballed her for most of last season. June had the last laugh though, when she proved her innocence and won first place against her accuser and, as luck would have it, Merry.

"Oh no, June's all in," Janice said. "And I'm really looking forward to seeing the both of you kick Emily's butt."

"That's not nice," Merry said, clicking her tongue and shaking her finger at her.

"Well, neither is she. She keeps referring to my retreat center as a dudette ranch." Janice folded her arms over her chest.

"What? Half the time this place is filled with men," Merry said.

"Exactly," Janice said, scowling. "Her father-in-law, Charlie, brings in really good business with the ex-cons that he's helping to rehabilitate into normal life."

"Yeah?" Merry said. "I saw a few new guys with Nate and Esteban when I came in. Are they ex-cons?"

Janice nodded. "They ride out with our ranch hands tomorrow. Today, they're being trained on what they need to do and what to expect."

"Have you ever had any trouble with the ex-cons?" Merry asked. It seemed a little dangerous to her, having guys just released from prison hanging around the property.

"No. As a matter of fact, I get more bullshit with the women's retreats than I do with the men. But that's probably because there are a couple of security guards that travel with Charlie's group to make sure that everybody plays nice." Janice grabbed two more cucumber slices and put them over her eyes again.

"Maybe you should try that with the women." Merry looked at the platter of vegetables that was laid out on the low table by the side of the hot tub and picked out a pepper slice to nibble on.

"Janice, are you in here?" a man's voice called from the front of the retreat center.

"Damn it." Janice scrambled out of the hot tub, the cucumber slices plopping back into the water. "That's Charlie. I forgot he needed to talk with me this afternoon. I'll be right back." She wrapped a plush cotton robe around her and hastily tied a knot in the sash.

Merry shrugged and picked up the cucumber slices as they floated over to her. Closing her eyes, she put them on over her lids. "More room for me," she said, sinking deeper into the hot tub. She was just fading into a nice light snooze when a deep, gravelly voice jolted her out of it.

"God bless Texas," a man said from the direction of the doorway.

Annoyed, Merry lifted a cucumber to glare at the intruder.

Holy shit. It was Simon Reynolds.

No, it couldn't be.

She sat up and stared at the man, trying to see the boy she once knew. Gone was the lean and lanky kid with the devil-may-care attitude who had stolen her heart. Simon had grown up rough, and it showed in his demeanor. He looked wary and poised to defend himself from an attack. Heavyset and muscled, Simon leaned a shoulder against the doorframe and stared at her in shock.

Did he hate her for abandoning him that night? Guilt washed over her, as fresh as if it had been ten hours ago instead of ten years.

His eyes were the same, a deep grayish blue, but there were a few lines around the corners of them. His sensual mouth looked just as kissable, but there was a tenseness about his jaw that was new. And she saw a hardness about him that hadn't been there when they had dated as teenagers. Her fingers itched to run through his shaggy black hair.

He looked as shocked as she did.

"What are you doing here?" Merry blurted out.

That was probably a rude thing to ask, but Simon had been in and out of prison for most of his life. The first time it had happened, though, Merry should have been right there with him. He had taken the rap and never even mentioned that she should have been indicted with him, even though she had no idea what he had been into.

Grand theft auto, larceny, breaking and entering—you name it. They would have thrown the book at her, even if they had believed her that she thought Simon had bought himself a Corvette at eighteen on a part-time ranch hand's salary. Or that the house they had been making love in didn't belong to him. She had been drunk on stolen booze from a Waterford crystal decanter, lying on a bearskin rug, wearing a diamond necklace that Simon had given her. That had been all she'd been wearing when the owner of the house, the booze, the rug, and the necklace had come back home early from his business trip.

"What are you doing here?" Simon asked hoarsely, looking everywhere but at her.

"You know me. I love hot tubs." They had used the hot tub that night as well.

He smirked, but still wouldn't meet her eyes. "I remember."

Simon had tackled the owner to keep him from shooting them. Merry had chucked off the necklace and grabbed her clothes. She had ducked into the changing room by the pool to get dressed. When she had heard gunshots, she'd nearly peed herself. Merry wasn't proud of it, but she ran for her life, leaving Simon behind. She had been barely eighteen at the time and they would have tried her as an adult, like they had him.

"What else do you remember?" she asked, tracing little circles in the water with her fingertips.

His face hardened into a stony mask and he finally stared into her eyes. She felt a tremor of excitement flutter through her. "It's been a while," he ground out.

"Little over ten years," she said. "Want to join me?" Merry stretched seductively. "We've got a lot of catching up to do."

That night, she had hitchhiked back home to her mother's trailer and had waited for the police to come and get her. They never did. Simon never called either. But she read about his arrest in the local paper. He had claimed the woman he was with was a call girl. They had believed him. Merry hadn't dared go to visit him or attend his trial. She had told her mother everything and Penny Grayson instantly turned against Simon, surprising Merry with the level of hatred Simon's name generated. Merry had a feeling that her mom was using Simon as a scapegoat of sorts. She couldn't take her frustrations about her own failed relationships out on the men who had left her, so Simon had become the target for Penny's rage.

"Sweetheart," he said, shaking his head. "You don't learn, do you?"

After he'd been sentenced, her mother had refused to let her visit him in prison. And at first, Merry had been too chicken to go alone. But she wrote him weekly. He never answered her letters or emails. She decided that she didn't want to risk the embarrassment of him not seeing her if she worked up the courage to walk into the prison for visiting hours.

The last thing Merry sent him was a postcard from New Mexico when she won her first All-Around. She had written one word on it: *Why?* Merry had wanted to know why he hadn't ratted her out. Or why he never contacted her when the coast was clear. She had thought they'd had something special. It had crushed her and she still felt some pangs of that abandonment even now.

"Sometimes I need things spelled out for me," Merry said.

Simon had responded to her postcard by sending her back a clipping of a newspaper article showing her riding Raphael, carrying the Texas flag. That still hadn't answered her questions, but she stopped trying to get him to reconnect with her after that. She could take a hint, eventually.

"It's not a good idea to get involved with men like me."

"Are you with Charlie's group?" she asked.

"You know Charlie?" he asked.

"Just by reputation."

"He's earned that reputation. Stay away from him, too." He took off his battered cowboy hat and ran his hand through his wavy hair.

"I think it's cute that you think you have any say in what I do. It's been ten years and you haven't said a word to me since that night," Merry said, levering herself to get out of the hot tub.

She could wait for answers on why he'd ghosted her all those years ago. But what she really wanted to see was if he was as good as she remembered, or if her teenage self had built up the fantasy in her head about his kisses. Because, so far, no other man had ever managed to compare to Simon, her first love.

"Don't," he croaked out, backing up several steps.

"Don't what?" She quirked an eyebrow at him.

"Merry, I've been in prison for five years. I've been out all of two days." He looked at her significantly. "I haven't been this close to a woman who was fully dressed in a long damned time, and you're only wearing a skimpy bathing suit."

She looked down at her one-piece suit. "This isn't skimpy. You should see the bikinis I usually wear."

Simon ran his hand down his face. "You could test the patience of a saint. And we both know I'm not one of those."

Never one to resist a challenge, Merry climbed out of the hot tub, dripping water and shaking out her hair seductively.

"I warned you," he said. Simon cleared the distance between them. Faster than she could guess, he hauled her into his arms and kissed her roughly.

It was like she was a teenager again. She hated that she had compared all of her other kisses to Simon's. He hadn't been her first boyfriend, but he was the one who taught her how to kiss. And in the ensuing ten years that they've been apart, it didn't seem like he'd lost his touch.

Damn, she had missed this. No one else had made her feel so wild and free.

She kissed him back eagerly. The hunger in him ignited something deep inside her belly. Holding on to him tightly, she ground against him. Simon clenched the back of her nylon bathing suit, and she knew if she had been wearing a bikini, he would've torn it off her already. She walked him back until he was pressed up against the wall of the retreat center. Moaning into his mouth, Merry reached out for his belt buckle as he gripped her hair in his fist.

"Simon?" a gruff male voice said. The sound of footsteps came closer. Simon thrust her away and took a couple of steps toward the end of the balcony. With his back to her, she saw him clutching the railing as he struggled to get his breathing under control. Normally, she would've felt bad for him. But he had abandoned her without a word for ten years and this was a little bit of payback. He had hurt her badly when he moved on as if they had been nothing to each other. Not to mention she was just as ready as he was to pick up where they'd left off all those years ago.

As she struggled to get her own breathing under control, Merry tangled her long blond hair into a sloppy braid and reveled at the throbbing wildness of her pulse. There was just something about a bad boy that made her senses sing. A few moments later, a tall, distinguished man walked out on the balcony and did a double take when he saw Merry. His hair was silver gray, but his eyes were a sharp green that saw everything. Handsome in a silver fox way, he was dressed like a ranch hand, but he moved like he was used to wearing four-digit designer suits. She'd bet her last dollar this was Charlie Lincoln, who was in charge of the ex-cons at Janice's retreat.

He nodded at her. "I hope we didn't disturb you, ma'am."

"Not at all," Merry said and held out her hand. "I'm Merry Grayson."

"I know who you are. I'm a big fan of you and your sister." He shook her hand. "I'm Charlie Lincoln."

Simon turned around and walked over to them. "Let's go," he said with a hand on Charlie's arm.

"You go on," Charlie said. "I want to talk to Merry for a bit."

Simon set his jaw and Merry thought for a moment he would refuse. But he gave Charlie a curt nod and stormed out of the retreat center.

"Is this where you tell me to stay away from the guys in your retreat?" Merry asked with a hand on her hip.

"As long as it's between consenting adults, I don't care." Charlie handed her one of the fluffy cotton robes and Merry gratefully put it on. There was nothing sexy about shivering after all.

"Janice and Trent are putting together quite the Christmas fundraiser," he said. "The barrel racing is sure to bring in a lot of people locally to see you and June go head-to-head."

"That's a lot of people who are going to see June lose," she said with a good-natured smile.

"She's going to give you a run for your money, and watching the two of you is going to be a hell of a lot of fun. I hear Trent is going to bring in some bucking broncs. LeAnn

Keller is going to come down as well."

That soured the shit out of her mood.

"That's very nice of her," Merry said between her teeth. It made sense, though. In addition to being her main competition in bronc busting, LeAnn "Killer" Keller was an upcoming rodeo star looking for publicity and sponsors. A former Miss Texas and a Dallas Rodeo Queen, LeAnn was everything the WPRC could want in an athlete. Unlike Shayna James, the WPRC's disgraced golden girl, LeAnn *wanted* to ride horses in the rodeo. And unlike Merry and June, she was a professional who kept her nose clean and promoted good, honest, wholesome family values. Her mother was her manager. Her father took care of her horses and traveled with them. She even had her two sisters on the road with her, though they didn't compete. It was one big happy family. Merry just wanted to barf when she thought about it.

"Think you and the Killer will go head-to-head in broncs?" Charlie asked.

The question set her teeth on edge. Her entire body screamed no. She needed a break. She hated that event. At the very least, she had planned to hold up until reality busted down the door in February when she had to compete.

But she needed the practice if her plan was to retire after she won the women's bronc-busting purse. In addition to LeAnn, there was other competition to worry about, younger girls who had trained in the sport long before it had become an official event in the WPRC. Merry was not used to being on an unruly horse, and had taken a lot of bumps and bruises while she learned bronc riding. At twenty-eight, she wasn't old by any stretch of the imagination, but her body didn't heal like it used to. And after several years of being on the circuit, her muscles and joints ached more than they did when she was younger.

"Absolutely," Merry said, letting her pride and ego take over her brain and tongue for the moment.

"Excellent," Charlie said. "It's going to be a good event. And with you and Killer on the posters, we're going to raise a lot of money for the underprivileged families of Last Stand."

That was the whole reason why she was doing this charity rodeo, after all. Unlike LeAnn, her family hadn't been all sunshine and roses, especially after the holidays when Luke skedaddled and the bills hit. If Merry could make someone's Christmas better, it didn't matter if the horse dumped her on her ass in front of hundreds of people or not.

"I'm sure I'll see you around," Charlie said. "And I know both you and Simon are adults…but he's got quite a road ahead of him. Maybe now is not the best time to start a relationship with him."

"Thanks for the warning," Merry said, and gave him a smile.

"Well, I tried." Charlie shook his head and then left.

Chapter Four

SIMON RESISTED THE urge to dunk his entire head inside the water trough. He could use a cold shower. He could use a kick in the ass. What he really could use was to march right back in the retreat center, throw Merry over his shoulder, and take her someplace private. Or not so private. He just wanted to take her.

Instead, he headed over to the barn where the rest of his group of parolees were saddling up. They were scheduled to take a quick tour of the back pastures and ride some of the land that they would be working for the next month.

Simon hadn't expected the gut punch of seeing Merry so soon. He certainly hadn't expected to see her dripping wet, wearing only a thin scrap of fabric. Simon closed his eyes and tried to will his body back under control. The last thing he wanted to do was ride several hours with a hard-on.

"All right, gentlemen," Nate Pierson, the Three Sisters Ranch's foreman said. "Saddle up. Half of you boys are going with Esteban. The other half are coming with me."

Even though Simon hadn't been on a horse in a decade, he hauled himself into the saddle by rote memory. The mare he was on was a brown Morgan horse, and he appreciated her calm and gentle nature. But he also stared at Nate's stallion with a little bit of envy. The horse was a mustang with an attitude. He could tell that Nate had him under tight control, as if the stallion would break out on his own if Nate was distracted for even a second.

Simon felt a great kinship to the horse. He just wanted to run full out, feel the wind in his hair, lift his hands over his head and scream, "I'm free." Instead, he held on to the reins and followed the rest the horses. Dipping his head back, he looked up at the endless blue sky. As they rode out through the acres of the Three Sisters Ranch, Simon was surprised to find a thread of anxiety coursing through him at the great wide open. So much of his life had been confined to a six-foot-square cell with only an hour or two each day spent outside of it.

He went into jail a stupid eighteen-year-old kid with a chip on his shoulder the size of Texas. And he got into trouble in prison, refusing to back down from fights. He'd had his nose broken more than once and after a really bad beating, he'd been hospitalized for broken ribs. But he had given as good as he got. He hadn't been an easy target and the predators found more simple prey. Because of that, though, he hadn't had any chance at early parole or release, even if he had been a first offender. Simon was pretty sure his father had had a hand in that as well. So Simon had done his five years and hadn't learned a damned thing. He should never have given in to temptation and stolen that Mercedes, but the keys had been in it and he had just wanted to go for a joyride. He wouldn't have sold it or delivered it to a chop shop. But in the end, the result was the same. His second five years was when he really grew up.

Simon's eyes continuously scanned around and behind him. Old habits died hard. The hairs on the back of his neck had been standing up because he sensed people behind him. Even though his mind knew they weren't a threat, he couldn't relax with the other members of the group at his back. It wasn't as if he thought they would attack him or anything. It was just that after a decade of always watching his six, he couldn't let himself drop his guard.

Nate pointed out the herds of cattle and the different pastures. He also showed them the fence posts that needed to be repaired, and other small jobs around the area that they would be responsible for in the upcoming week. At least being a ranch hand hadn't changed in the years since he had been in prison. Animals needed to be fed. Fences needed to be repaired. Plants needed to be weeded and watered. Shit needed to be shoveled.

He had worked on farms and ranches most summers when he'd been growing up...and his father hadn't given a shit about where he was. Simon had loved working outdoors after being cooped up in high school all year—when he bothered to show up.

Now, a part of him wanted to run back inside and hide in a cell without any windows. He knew the routine there. He didn't have a lot of choices to make and the consequences of fucking up were immediate and memorable. Out here, he could do anything he wanted. The sad fact was, he had no idea what that was.

All in all, they were only out about three hours, but it felt like an eternity. Simon kept waiting for the dream to end, and he'd wake up in his cell. His prison life was over though. Now, he had to figure out what to do with his normal life.

When they got back to the Three Sisters Ranch, Simon looked around for a sign of Merry, but he didn't see her. He knew it was silly to think that she would wait for him, and want to pick up where they'd left off. He wondered where she was and if maybe he could track her down.

Nate and Esteban showed them how to take care of the horses and the equipment. This was something that he had done when he was in high school, so he only listened with half an ear as his mind wandered back to the past.

Simon couldn't help but wonder when he looked at Esteban and Nate... If his father hadn't had him arrested, would he be working at a ranch like they were? He certainly wouldn't have become a corporate bigwig like his daddy, or followed in his corrupted footsteps. Braxton had worked in a venture capitalist firm and he'd wheeled and dealt with the best of them. And he'd also taken bribes and crushed careers. But as long as Braxton got paid, he hadn't cared whose lives he had ruined, least of all his wife's and son's.

In the two days before Simon had to report into the retreat center, he'd gone to check out his mother's little cabin...and had found it unlivable. It was a shame to see what the years of neglect had done to it. He cleaned it up the best that he could, but it needed new plumbing and some rewiring before he could stay there.

Since he needed all his funds for the repair work, he

hadn't a choice but to return to the scene of the crime—literally. His father's mansion had been upkept and like a time capsule, it looked almost exactly the same as it had ten years ago, when his father had had him arrested in it. Simon had slept poorly there and had been glad when it was time to report to the ranch. The only bright side about the house was the Corvette had also been there. And it had been in pristine condition.

"Well, that's it. Any questions?" Nate asked.

No one in his group had any.

"All right. I suggest you get yourself settled into the guesthouse. Dinner is at six p.m. tonight. And we will have an early start tomorrow morning at four a.m."

Nate paused as if he was awaiting groans and complaints. He seemed a bit surprised when he didn't get any. These men were used to doing what they were told. Getting up at four in the morning was a small price to pay for not having bars around the doors and windows.

Simon's group were all out on parole. All of them had paid for their crimes. None of them were murderers or rapists or violent offenders. But he still wouldn't want to cross any one of them. The one thing they had in common was that they all had spent several years in prison. Some of them he knew from his cell block. Others were from another prison.

When everyone dispersed, Simon headed for the parking lot and his car. He would come back to the guesthouse to sleep, but right now, he needed to go for a drive. He was overjoyed when he saw Merry lying down on the roof of his purple Corvette. Unfortunately, she was dressed in a long skirt and a T-shirt instead of the sexy little bathing suit with the Texas flag on it. She had thrown her arm over her eyes and seemed to be taking a nap.

"Hey! If you scratch my paint job, I'll take it out on your hide," he said. Didn't the Three Sisters Ranch have any lounge chairs she could have used?

Merry sat up and blinked at him with her big, beautiful blue eyes. "Please tell me this is not the same car you got arrested for stealing."

"Recognize it?" He scared her off the hood when he clicked the alarm to open up the locks. "Want to go for a ride?" He drawled the question, hoping his double entendre was coming through loud and clear.

Apparently, it had, because she smiled back at him wickedly and said, "I was hoping you'd ask."

"Like there was a doubt?" He opened the door for her, and she slid in.

He admired her long, toned legs that flashed at him through the slit in her ankle-length skirt. His body was throbbing to attention again. Simon hoped that he had enough in him to make it to a bed this time, but he was ready to take her in the car if she was willing. Getting behind the wheel, he started the Corvette up. The powerful roar of the engine settled something deep inside him.

He loved this car. He had always loved this car. His father had bought this car as a fuck you to Simon, who'd refused to visit his father after the man ran away with Joyce, his secretary, leaving his mother heartbroken and suicidal.

"Hang on," Simon said. He backed out of the parking lot, spewing gravel. Taking off fast down the long driveway of the Three Sisters Ranch, he kept his foot on the gas, egged on by Merry's laughter. He would do anything to keep hearing that.

"Slow down," she shrieked with joy. "I'm pretty sure getting charged with speeding is a violation of your parole."

"Spoilsport," he said. But she was right, and he jacked it back down to the limit. Just in time too, as they passed by Police Chief Highwater in his squad car at the edge of town.

"Where are we going?" Merry asked.

"Scene of the crime," he said.

"That's not funny." She socked him in the arm.

"No, but there's a sense of coming full circle."

"Simon, we don't have to go there. I'm staying at the Last Stand Bed-and-Breakfast."

He looked over at her in confusion. "Why aren't you staying with your family?"

Merry made a face. "My sister April is shacking up with someone, and they're in the 'banging on every open surface' phase of their relationship. June's staying at my mom's trailer and brings Esteban home for a roll in the hay every time my mother steps out to go shopping. Besides, I like my own space. It has privacy, a pool in the back, and wireless internet. I might never leave."

"We can go there another time."

"There's going to be another time?"

"Unless you tell me no," he said.

"There are a few conversations I'd like to have first."

Merry leaned in and placed a hand high up on his thigh.

It took all of his concentration to keep the wheel steady on the road. This had to be a dream. He couldn't believe that she was here, next to him after all these years.

"What do you want to talk about?" he asked, hearing how hoarse his voice sounded. If he was a decent man, he'd be taking her to a diner to have a cup of coffee or something. Instead, the pure lust that was driving him could only think of losing himself in her soft, sweet body.

"Why didn't you answer any of my letters?"

Simon shook his head. It had been hard not to. He had been so lonely, but he couldn't let her wait for him.

"Did you even read them?" she asked sadly.

He reached out and took her hand. "Of course I did."

"Were you mad at me for not coming forward and admitting to my part in the robbery?"

Squeezing her hand, Simon said, "No. Not at all. There was nothing for you to confess to."

"I think I was aiding and abetting, or at least an accomplice."

"None of that. I never wanted the ugly business to touch you."

She held his hand tight, just like they had done when they were dating. "Maybe if there was another person to blame, your sentence wouldn't have been so long."

"It was a done deal as soon as my daddy came back early from his business trip."

"What did your father have to do with anything?"

Simon felt Merry stiffen next to him as she recognized

where they were. He punched in the key code that opened the gates and pulled the sportscar down the long driveway that led to his father's mansion.

"You don't have to do this to impress me," she said quietly. "Let's just go before somebody notices us."

"No one's going notice us. It's just you and me."

Merry's laugh sounded hollow. "That's what you said last time."

"This time, there's not going to be an old man shooting .22 rounds all over the house and threatening to kill us." He parked the car in front of the main doors of the mansion.

"How can you be so sure?" Merry asked.

Simon turned off the car. "Because he's dead." He got out of the car.

She gaped at him while he walked around the hood to open the door for her. He held out his hand and helped her out of the low-slung car.

"Did you kill him?" she asked.

"I would have, but I didn't. Cancer got to the bastard before I could."

"I don't think that's any better." Merry let him lift her up out of the car and he held her against him, briefly. Too briefly.

"I'll explain it all inside."

Merry let out a sigh. "I've got a lot of questions."

"And I got answers for you." Opening the door, Simon disabled the security alarm. Of course, he had done the same thing ten years ago, so he didn't blame her when she continued to look at him suspiciously. He locked the door behind them, and leaned back against it as she stared around the foyer.

"It hasn't changed a bit," she said.

"He didn't live here much, even when he was alive." He brushed by her and walked into the sumptuous living room. "Can I get you a drink?" Simon went to the bar and poured himself three fingers of whiskey from a crystal decanter. When he looked back, Merry was shaking her head at him.

"It's like déjà vu."

"Not quite," he said. "You're wearing too many clothes."

She walked over to him, bold as brass, and he couldn't look away from the soft curves that her T-shirt and long silky skirt did nothing to hide. Taking the whiskey in the Baccarat cut glass out of his hand, she tossed back a healthy swallow and handed it back.

"It's still the good stuff. Okay, we've done it. Now let's get out here before we get caught."

"We haven't done it yet." He grinned.

"You can't seriously expect me to have sex with you in a stranger's house—again, after driving here in a perhaps stolen car."

"The car's mine."

She looked at him suspiciously.

"I can show you the papers."

"Who owns this house?" Merry demanded.

"I do," he said. "And I can show you those papers too, but they're upstairs in the safe."

"I don't want to doubt you," she said. "But you always were a very good bullshit artist. Can you tell me how the hell you can afford a Corvette and this house?" She crossed her arms over her magnificent breasts.

He was distracted, but who could blame him? Merry Grayson, one of the wild Grayson sisters, rodeo champ and the last woman he took his time and made love to, was standing two feet in front of him. The fact he wasn't already inside of her should have qualified him for a gold medal in restraint.

"Don't tell me you won the lottery or some other nonsense."

"I inherited both when my father died."

"That was the second lie I thought you'd say." She scowled at him. "Lottery or a rich uncle. How dumb do you think I am?"

"I don't think you're dumb at all. I think you're beautiful."

Simon wondered if her mouth would taste like whiskey. He decided to give it a try. It was easy to step in close to her, thread his fingers through her long, blond hair and bring her in for a kiss.

Merry wrapped her arms around him, but he hadn't expected her tongue to meet his seductive dance. Simon groaned deeply and slid his other hand down to her ass and cupped the sweet curve of it. The kiss was as sexy and as sweet as he remembered. He would gleefully never take another breath, but when she tore her mouth away, he took in a few ragged ones.

"Sweetheart," he groaned. "It's been five long years since I've been with a woman. And it wasn't even that good. Even before that, you were the only one I wanted. If you don't want to have sex, right here and right now, you better run."

Merry unbuttoned his pants and slid down the zipper.

"I'll take that to mean that you are not going anywhere." And he kissed her again.

She reached inside his pants and took his hard-on in her soft grip. Simon didn't know what good deed he'd ever done to deserve this, but as she rubbed him slowly while his mouth made love to her, he made a note to do it again and again.

It was no contest. He was going to come hard before this even got started. He thought briefly of moving away, but she felt too good in his arms. Her sweet kisses and caresses were driving him to the brink and all too soon, he came with a release that shattered him and made him weak in the knees.

Reluctantly Simon took his lips off hers. "Now, look what you made me do. I'm a mess." He shrugged out of his shirt and tossed it aside, still shaking from the aftereffects of his orgasm.

Merry traced little tiny circles all over his abdomen. Every crunch he did in prison, every weight he lifted, was worth it to see the raw desire in her eyes as she touched him. She reached behind them to grab the whiskey decanter and the glasses. Then she sashayed out to the balcony porch. Over her shoulder she said, "Now, about those answers…"

Chapter Five

MERRY FINISHED THE whiskey in her glass and poured them both two more. She couldn't remember being this turned on in a long while. When Simon followed her out, he ignored the whiskey glass that she offered him, and turned her around so that she faced the beautiful view of the Texas landscape. She held on to the balcony rail and looked out at the wide rolling acres in front of her.

There was no way he'd inherited this. Did he think she was born yesterday?

"You're wearing too many clothes," he growled in her ear. Her nipples were already pebbled hard and her panties completely wet, but the sound of his voice took everything up a notch. Pulling her T-shirt over her head, Simon took in a deep breath. Merry expected her bra to be next, but was completely surprised when he pulled her back around to face him.

"Who put those marks on your body?"

In that instant, Simon was no longer the sexy bad boy she had lost her heart to. Instead, she saw the ravages of prison time in his cold gray eyes.

"W-what?" she stuttered.

This man was a dangerous stranger. A lot could happen to a person in ten years, especially when those years were spent in prison. Her mama always said she never had a lick of sense. Merry had driven off with an ex-con because of a girlhood crush, and now she was possibly going to pay the price for that.

Except this was Simon. Her Simon. Even though the last ten years had been rough on him, deep down he was still the same person. He had always been wildly protective of her. Merry just wasn't used to a man giving a damn on that level.

"I want to know who put those marks on your body. You don't have to be afraid of him anymore."

"Marks?" That gave her pause. What the hell was he talking about? His intensity took her breath away, but as she really took a good look at him, she realized he wasn't going to hurt her. Then clarity hit.

"Are you kidding me?" she asked, pushing him back hard with the palms of her hands. He barely moved. "Are you determined to go back to jail?" She clutched his arms as tightly as he was gripping her upper arms and tried to shake him, but he was immovable.

"The name, Merry."

"Well, the purple one on my shoulder blade was made by Cisco. And the bruise in the middle of my back that radiates down to my tailbone was done by Tinkerbell."

Simon blinked at her.

"They're horses, jackass. Broncs."

Simon released her and took a step back, rubbing his hands over his face. "Who names a wild horse Tinkerbell?"

"Someone with a real crazy sense of humor."

"I'm sorry about that," he said quietly and snagged the whiskey glass off the railing.

"I wouldn't kill them, though, if I were you," Merry continued. "They cost a couple thousand dollars each. But if you really feel the need, you could probably punch Tinkerbell out for me. She was a nasty bitch. It was bad enough that she threw me. She back-kicked and almost took my head clean off."

"I didn't think," he said, looking up. "In prison, bruising like that meant someone had worked you over. Fresh bruises meant someone was still doing it. I should've thought before I reacted. I got into a lot of fights in prison—that's why I didn't get an early release."

"Even if it had been a man who did this to me," she said, cupping his face, "you can't do anything that would risk your parole. Getting into a fight could definitely cost you another five years or more of freedom. I don't want you to do that for me again."

"I didn't do time for you before," he said.

"You did. By refusing to name the woman you were with, you saved me from, at the very least, having a rather nasty conversation with my mother and the chief of police."

"That would have been the best-case scenario. My father was out for blood. He wanted to punish anyone and everyone involved."

"Again, what does your father have to do with what happened?"

Simon gestured all around him. "I stole my father's car,

that's true. We didn't break and enter, though. The reason I had the codes was because I had a bedroom upstairs. This was my father's love nest, the place where he brought his mistresses."

"What?" she screeched. What the absolute fuck? This was too crazy. She'd almost believe the lottery story over this. And yet, Simon's voice rang with sincerity and his eyes held the ghosts of past hurts. This wasn't bullshit, no matter how much she wished it was. "This is your dad's place? That asshole shooting at us was your father?"

"Yup. Back then, he had joint custody of me, but I couldn't stand to be in the same house with him and his lover du jour. The one my mother divorced him over was named Joyce. He married her before the ink on the divorce papers dried. She was twenty-three—five years older than me at the time. My mother didn't take the betrayal well. She took him for what she could. Then she fell down the bottom of a whiskey bottle and eventually drank herself to death while I was in prison."

"I'm so sorry."

He nodded. "Me too."

"That's awful." Merry shook her head, feeling sick to her stomach.

Slinging himself into a chair, Simon said, "So was my father. He and Joyce deserved each other."

"So, let me get this straight. We were fooling around in your father's house, where you had every right to be?" Merry brought over the decanter and her glass, sitting across from him at a white wicker side table. She was aware that she was wearing nothing but a bra and her skirt, but Simon seemed miles away. He wordlessly accepted a refill, and they clinked glasses.

"Yup."

"That's messed up. I can't believe your father actually pressed charges against you." Merry's father would never win any Father of the Year awards, but Luke had at least paid child support every now and then when he remembered he had a daughter.

"Whenever I was here, and my father was gone on business trips, Joyce was a bitch to me." He drank deep. "I suppose I didn't make it easy for her, either."

"She seems like a real piece of work. Sleeping with a married man. Being a jerk to his kid. Where is your step-monster now? I want to go beat the shit out of her," Merry said.

"Hey, if I can't beat the shit of anybody, you can't either."

"I can make it look like an accident." Merry tapped her cheek thoughtfully.

Simon smirked. "I don't know where she is and I don't care. Anyway, the night we got caught, Joyce was at her boyfriend's place. I'm not sure if my father knew about it or cared. He had other side pieces as well. So I thought the coast was clear."

"Did you ever wonder why he let you go to prison?" Merry was still having trouble wrapping her head around that. His own son!

"Not only did he let me go to prison, he made sure that the judge threw the book at me. It was a travesty. I was a first-time offender, at least as far as the courts knew. I was barely eighteen, but they tried me as an adult and sentenced me as if I was a risk to society. To be fair, I had been stealing his bimbo's jewelry and hocking it. I kept some of the money for myself, as you probably figured out. Taking pretty girls out on dates isn't cheap, you know."

"See, I was an accomplice or an accessory. I get those two mixed up."

"I donated a bunch of the money to charities that he hated: domestic violence shelters, food kitchens, social services, that type of thing."

"You were like a modern-day Robin Hood," she said.

"Exactly. And he couldn't afford to let those donations get out to the media. It would destroy his reputation with his power base. It was better that he had a troubled son in jail, than to have the world know he'd made his son so vengeful that the kid felt forced to give all his money to charities to make amends for his father being such a douchebag." Simon gave a short mocking laugh. "He always thought I was a thug and no good. He probably thought that prison would make a man out of me. Or at least make me weak enough that I would accept his total control over my life." Simon gestured to the house. "I've got half a mind to donate the proceeds when I sell this monstrosity as well."

"I can see why you would feel that way," Merry said. "But I think your father owes you restitution for what he did to you. This house could be it."

Simon nodded. "Probably. It's just that I don't want a damned thing from him. But the irony of this house being mine is something I want to savor for a bit longer."

"Do you think Joyce will challenge the will?"

"The old man divorced her about two years into my sentence. He must have paid her off good, because her name didn't even come up when I talked with the executors of the estate. He never remarried after Joyce. And from what people tell me, he died alone."

"Do you feel guilty about that?"

Simon made a rude noise. "Hell no. For one, I was still in jail at the time. I could've gone to the funeral, though. But I figured, why bother? He'd alienated every other human being who had ever come in contact with him. I say karma got him in the end more than the cancer did. He fucked up my life. I was a rebellious kid who'd been sent to prison. I don't know what they expected me to learn in there, but whatever it was, I didn't learn it. When I came out the first time, I had a bad attitude and my choices led me right back in."

"What happened?"

"I stole another car. I was stupid. So stupid. But that's not going to happen again."

Merry believed him. "It must've been so hard on you, to be there all alone. Why didn't you let me help?"

"You did help. I read your letters over and over. They were my one bright spot in an otherwise terrible place and terrible time."

"Why didn't you ever write me back, then?" Merry tried to keep the hurt out of her voice. She had thought all these years he had forgotten her, had forgotten them.

"The same reason why I never mentioned you during the trial. You were a rising star on the rodeo circuit. You couldn't afford to have your reputation ruined by being connected with me."

"That wouldn't have mattered to me. It still doesn't."

"It mattered to me. It was satisfying to me that my father couldn't touch you. I loved reading about you competing and how you and your sister June became the wild Grayson sisters. You became an entertainer, as well as an athlete. I was very proud of you. I still am."

Merry blinked back tears. She didn't think anyone had ever told her that.

"I didn't want anyone to use me as a way to dim your star. That wasn't going to happen. Not on my watch."

"And how about now?" she asked.

"I think we should keep this on the down low. I don't think people on social media would be very kind to you if they found out you were dating an ex-con."

"Ask me if I care." She crossed her arms and glared at him.

"I care. Merry, we haven't talked in ten years. Obviously, the chemistry is still there and I want you like hell. I admire you and I want the best for you. But I'm no good for you."

Rolling her eyes, she resisted the urge to curse at him. "Why don't you let me decide what's good for me or not?"

"I don't have the strength to resist you right now," he said. "But I know you're going to come to your senses sooner or later."

"Fine. Let's take this one day at a time while we make up

for lost time. Who knows what could have happened if your father hadn't been such a dick. We were going hot and heavy, maybe we would've burned out. Or maybe, it could have gotten more serious." Her heart trembled at the thought. He could have been hers all this time.

"I can't do serious right now," he said. "Like I said, it's been a bit of a whirlwind. I just got out on parole, and found out that I have a house and a Corvette, when I thought I'd have to live in my mom's cabin."

"I remember that cabin," she said as memories of their dates there brought a smile to her face.

"You wouldn't recognize it now," he said. "I'm trying to get some contractors in to fix up the place, but I'm going to run out of money."

"Your father was broke?"

"I'm not touching his money. He ruined too many people's lives making it. Including my mother's."

"Then isn't it justice that his money fixes up her cabin?" Merry asked.

"I don't know. I'd rather be homeless."

"That's pride talking."

"Maybe it is. I wasn't expecting this…" He gestured with his hand. "I thought I was going to spend the next month trying to get my head on straight at the retreat center. Now, I've got to figure out what I'm going to do with the rest of my life."

"I can understand that," she said, thinking about her own decision to retire after winning the bronc-busting event. "What do you want to do?"

"Not go back to jail."

"That one seems easy enough. What else?" She tried to remember back when they were kids. Had they ever talked about the future?

"I want to put my past behind me."

"That's not so easy," she said.

"Tell me about it. Things are a lot more complicated than I imagined."

"Am I one of those complications?" Merry asked.

"No. You're a sight for sore eyes."

"Even though you and I have some unfinished business with each other?"

"Monkey business, maybe." He leaned in and kissed her.

The familiar burn started up in her again and she wanted him more than anything she had ever wanted in her entire life. Her one true love was right here and she wasn't sure how this was going to end. It could go up in flames or it could be everything she had dreamed of. Suddenly, she was scared. There hadn't been a man in her life who hadn't left her high and dry once they got sick of her bullshit. Her father had left. Simon had left. Men came in and out of her life all the time. Zane had flown off to Tahiti without her, and they had only ever been friends.

Simon hadn't wanted to leave. Not back then. What if he left now? Where would she be if her first and only love decided she wasn't worth sticking around for?

"I'm not asking you to marry me. I'm just asking you to have fun with me," Merry said when he lifted his mouth from hers. They could start off slow, get to know each other as adults. See if they still had the magic they used to have when they were together.

"That I can do."

"So let's have fun." Merry undid her bra and tossed it on the table between them.

"Have mercy," he drawled.

"Not a chance." She walked over to him and straddled his legs. "Now, where were we?" She stroked her fingers through his hair.

"When?"

"All those years ago."

Merry yelped when he stood up, securing his hands under her ass. She hitched up her skirt and wrapped her legs around his waist.

"I believe we were in front of the fire." Simon carried her back into the living room and laid her down on the bearskin rug. "Get your clothes off. I'll start the fire."

"You've already got some good wood there," she joked as she shimmied out of her panties and skirt.

"Heh," he said, turning on the gas fireplace.

She appreciated the warmth. It was a chilly December in Texas and she had just been outside in her bra and a thin skirt.

"Damn, you're beautiful," he said, shucking off his clothes.

"Are you sure the door is locked?" Merry said, half-seriously.

"No one is going to interrupt this. You're all mine tonight."

"Have mercy," she whispered at the intense expression in his eyes as he knelt between her legs.

"Not a chance," he said, and spread her legs wide. "Looks like you're already wet for me."

"Condoms?" she gasped out as he lowered his mouth to her inner thigh and kissed it.

"Your sweet hand job gave me the wherewithal to take my time a bit. I can't tell you how much I thought about tasting you again. Which is good because I didn't think I'd need to go to the drugstore anytime soon. So unfortunately, I don't have any condoms."

"I've got a box in my purse." She pointed to where she dropped it on the couch.

"Good to know." Simon smiled at her and then lay between her legs and licked her slowly.

Hands grasping at the rug, Merry's eyes rolled back in pleasure. She hadn't expected him to take his time like this. Each flick of his tongue made her eager for the hard loving that she thought was in store for her. Raising her hips up to meet his mouth, she sighed when he tongued her faster, brushing over her clit.

"Yeah, just like that," she said, as he pressed closer.

Holding her to him, he alternated licking and sucking on her until she was dizzy from the pleasure. The slow burn that had teased her now roared like an inferno as she bucked and writhed. Simon eagerly lapped at her, not letting her twist away from the rampaging orgasm that crashed down on her. Twitching and shivering as each touch brought her pleasure so sharp it was almost too much, Merry came gripping the back of his head and rubbing herself all over his face.

"Fuck," she breathed, falling back to the rug.

"Eventually." Simon kissed up her belly until he got to her breasts.

His big body pressing down on her, he took her tight, sensitive nipple into his mouth and sucked hard while fondling the other one. Merry could feel his hard cock against her inner thigh and she wanted it inside her, but Simon would not be moved. He lavished her breasts with kisses and long strokes of his tongue.

"You're driving me crazy," she gritted out.

"Good," he said, then his mouth finally covered hers.

Distracted by his kiss, she missed the chance to ease the ache between her thighs by coaxing him inside her. But Simon didn't disappoint. His fingers thrust in and fucked her slowly while he made love to her mouth.

It was so much different from the last time. Back then, they'd eagerly explored each other's bodies, giving and taking, having all the time in the world to go from orgasm to orgasm. Now, there was an urgency in his frantic fingers and deep kisses. As if despite his words, he was afraid they would be interrupted.

Rubbing his arms and shoulders, Merry tried to go lower to stroke him, but he was just out of reach. He left her mouth and she gasped in air when he buried his face against her neck while he sucked and nibbled on her sweet spot there.

He remembered everything that pleased her. His hands were everywhere, inside her, on her breasts. "Get the condoms," she said raggedly.

"Come on my fingers," he said, leaning up on an elbow to look down at her.

She held on to his shoulders and rode them.

"That's my cowgirl." Simon hooked his fingers and hit that spot. Her heels pressed into the floor and she nearly came out of her skin.

He swallowed her shout with another blistering kiss and she pumped her hips as the second orgasm rolled through her, as if she was being tossed around on an ocean wave.

Spent, Merry collapsed into a puddle of goo. Her legs felt like rubber and her entire body throbbed with pleasure. Simon nipped gently at her chin. "Now, I'll get the condom."

In a daze, she watched his fine ass as he went over to her purse and pulled out the box of condoms. Kneeling by her, he said, "Put it on me."

With shaking fingers, it took a few tries to get the package open. Before she rolled it on, she leaned down and licked the tip. Simon grabbed her hair and said, "Don't stop now."

Grinning, she pushed him down on the rug. Placing the condom next to her, she gripped his thick cock in her hand and cupped his balls. Swirling her tongue around the tip, Merry let her long hair fall over his stomach and legs.

She rubbed his cock between her breasts and then licked the tip.

"Damn that's a sight," he said shakily.

She worked him with her hand while going wet and wild on him with her tongue. Hollowing out her cheeks, she sucked him hard, wanting him as frantic for her as she was for him. She got into a rhythm that made him grunt and thrust up into her. She took him deep and then almost let him slide out.

"I'm going to come," he said, his body trembling.

She picked up the pace, sliding him in and out of her mouth. He cradled her face, his hips twitching, his body taut. Simon came with a tortured grunt and lay panting as she eased him out of her mouth and into the condom.

"Fuck," he said.

"It's time." She straddled his hips and pushed his still-hard cock inside her. Then she settled down on top of him. This type of bucking bronc was exactly what she needed. Simon played with her bouncing breasts as she found the pace and angle to get her to another orgasm. He was thick and hard, and felt so good as he filled her. Bracing her palms on his shoulders, she looked into his glazed eyes and knew he was going to come again.

Good.

Because so was she.

His hips pistoned up to meet each downward thrust. He clutched her hips as they pounded into each other. Her hair flying, Merry arched back, taking him deep.

"Yes," she whispered as his body and hers slammed together and came apart. All her aches and pains were forgotten. All her worries about the rodeo and being home for Christmas faded away. There was just this. The primal mating of two wild hearts.

"Yes," he snarled, pushing himself up.

No longer content to be on the bottom, Simon rolled to his feet, their bodies still joined. He walked to the nearest wall. Stretching her hands over her head, Merry moaned as he took control. She was being held up by his thrusts as she locked her ankles around his back.

The friction was sweet. The speed was thrilling, and the hard pounding was exactly what she wanted and needed. Merry wasn't sure who came first, but she clamped down on him and let the sweet release drench them both with pleasure.

"I can't feel my legs," she said, sagging against him.

"Don't worry. I'll carry you." Simon brought them back to the rug. After taking care of the condom, he joined her.

They stroked each other and kissed as the sweat cooled off their bodies. Merry was getting drowsy, but she didn't want to sleep on the floor.

"Shall we take this upstairs with the decanter of whiskey?" she asked, pushing the hair from his eyes.

Simon groaned. "I'd love to, but I've got to get back to the Three Sisters Ranch."

"Why?" Merry asked, stretching out in front of the fire. It felt good against her aches and pains that were starting to come back now that the adrenaline had worn off.

"I hate it here. As you can imagine, this place doesn't have the best of memories."

"I'll be here with you." She rubbed his arm.

"Yeah, but eventually you'd fall asleep and then it would just be me and my fucked-up head reliving the past ten years. I'd rather be at the retreat center with the other guys."

"Even if that means getting up at four in the morning and working in the hot sun all day?" Merry's brow crinkled in confusion.

"That retreat was a condition of my parole. And anyway, I'm not afraid of hard work. It's good to get back on a horse again."

Merry couldn't argue with him about that. Although the last thing she'd want to do was get back on a horse right now. She was sore as hell, and not from the fantastic love-making they had just indulged in. She looked around the large living room. "You should make new memories here. You could really go all out decorating for Christmas in a place like this. I bet you could easily get a twelve-footer in here. I think it would look great in that corner." She pointed.

"Sounds like a lot of work. Especially in a place that I'm not going to spend more than a few hours in."

"Maybe if you made it look a little more homey or personal, you'd feel differently. Make it your own, instead of your father's."

"I doubt it," he said, scowling at the place. "It's going on the market in the new year. I don't suppose you want to buy it?"

Merry shook her head. "I grew up in a trailer that could fit in this living room. What the heck would I do with all this space?"

"Exactly. I lived in a six-foot-by-six-foot room, so you can imagine what all this space feels like to me."

"Did you ever spend Christmas here?"

"Not if I could help it. Can you imagine a twenty-three-year-old stepmom, an eighteen-year-old boy, and a fifty-five-year-old man trying to make cozy Christmas memories, while my mother was slowly drinking herself to death because her perfect family had been ruined, simply because her husband couldn't keep it in his pants? Christmas is just another day. I'll probably get some Chinese food and take in a movie."

Merry's heart broke for him. She could hear the hurt underneath that statement. His parents were gone. He had been an only child, and it sounded like he wasn't close with any other relatives. "You're welcome to celebrate Christmas with us," Merry said. "I'm not sure if we're all going to crowd into the trailer or if April and Cole had something planned at their place."

Simon shook his head. "I'm not big on family gatherings."

And her mother probably still hated him. But that was a problem for another day. Merry wasn't about to let this one go, but she knew that now was not the time to push it. Not when the ghost of his father and all the memories were bearing down on him.

"I'll take a ride back with you to the Three Sisters Ranch instead of catching an Uber," she said. "I need to check in on my horse, and my truck is in the parking lot there anyway."

"Of course, you're riding with me. I wouldn't have it any other way."

They got cleaned up and dressed. Merry wondered why she felt out of sorts. Maybe it was because she half-expected him to disappear for another ten years. Every man in her life had ended up abandoning her at some point. She was a lot to handle. She knew that.

On the way back to the ranch, she asked, "I know you're here for a month for the retreat and to get acclimated back into society. I glanced at Charlie Lincoln's pamphlet. Do you have any plans for afterward?"

"Nothing set in stone. If I like what I'm doing on the ranch, I may look for a ranch-hand job somewhere."

"When you sell that house, you can pretty much set yourself up anywhere and do anything you want, at least for a couple of years."

"I haven't thought that far ahead. I'm still trying to process that the old man left me the house and the car. It almost makes me wish I talked to him that one last time when he came to visit."

"Why didn't you?" Merry asked.

"I didn't want to hear his apology. And even more, I was afraid that he wasn't going to apologize. Does that make sense?"

"It does. Don't beat yourself up over it. I'm sure he was remorseful for what he did to you."

"I'm not." Simon snorted.

"Even still, you had the right to protect yourself by not talking with him."

"The last time I spoke to him," Simon said, "was the day I surrendered myself. I think the old man thought I would be begging for leniency after a few days. That didn't happen. Then I think he thought that once I got out, I would come running back to him for forgiveness. And when that didn't happen either, I think he knew that he'd lost his son for good. I never opened his letters and I never contacted him again."

That was pretty bleak. If her father had tried that hard, Merry would have talked to him. Then again, her father hadn't shot at her or sent her to jail. Since all her sisters had different fathers, it had seemed normal for hers not to stick around. But hers never sent letters, just the odd birthday card or postcard. Enough to let her know she had been in his thoughts, no matter how briefly. She often wondered if it had been because of his wandering spirit…or the fact that he didn't want her and her mother in his life.

It didn't help that Luke only seemed to come around just after she'd won a big championship or title. When she had lost, though, he wasn't to be found. It had been up to her mother and sisters to get her through the little failures she had experienced.

Simon dropped her off by the barn when they got back to the Three Sisters Ranch. Leaning in to kiss him, Merry asked, "Can I see you tomorrow?"

"I'm not sure what I'm going to have left in me, but hell yeah." He kissed her.

"Let's take this a day at a time," she suggested. Merry didn't want to spook him.

"All right," he said. He held on to her longer than she thought he would. "You're amazing, you know? And you were everything I had dreamed about."

"Oh honey," she whispered in his ear. "We're just getting

started."

Christmas wouldn't be so dull with Simon around. Sure, it wasn't Tahiti, but Simon Reynolds had always been a good time. And she couldn't resist the chance to relive the best of her teenage years with him a bit, without the getting shot at portion.

Chapter Six

NOT SURPRISINGLY, SIMON had the best night's sleep of his life. He wasn't even mad when the alarm went off at three thirty a.m. He lay in bed and stared up at the ceiling, though, wondering where the hell he was. Then as the sounds of the other inmates—no, other members of the retreat—filtered in, he remembered. The joy and relief nearly overwhelmed him. He was out. He was free.

Since he had showered last night, he let his roommate, Chris, use the bathroom first. They had a hell of a day ahead of them. Torn between excitement and nervousness, Simon went to his bureau and picked out his clothes—no more orange jumpsuits in a sturdy, stiff canvas. Thick socks would protect his feet from his brand-new cowboy boots that he had splurged on. The soft cotton T-shirt he slipped on felt like silk. Getting dressed in a comfortable pair of jeans and T-shirt was a luxury Simon didn't think he'd ever take for granted again. While he waited for his turn in the bathroom, Simon opened the window shades and peered out at the ranch. It was still dark out, but it was a luminescent dark. He could see the hint of dawn that was softening the edges of the night as it faded into day.

Deciding he could wait a bit to brush his teeth, Simon went downstairs, feeling the pull of freedom. He kept expecting someone to stop him or call him back when he walked out the front door of the retreat. The early morning air felt like a caress as he walked over to the bunkhouse where the ranch hands lived. He could see lights on there.

As much as he liked the solitude of the morning, it raised the hair on his arms. He wasn't used to quiet. Quiet in prison meant some serious shit was about to go down. Simon hoped that feeling would pass, but for right now, so soon out of prison, he had to remember to be patient. He had ten years of conditioning to overcome.

One of the ranch hands, Frenchie—Simon remembered—stepped out onto the porch and lit a cigarette. Frenchie nodded at him as he approached.

"Coffee's not ready yet," he said. "Give it another ten minutes."

"No problem." Simon was surprised at how loud his voice sounded in the emerging dawn.

"Cigarette?" Frenchie offered.

"Gave it up," Simon said. It had been an expensive habit, and he had found a better use for them as currency instead. Still, the scent was familiar and he didn't mind the smoke.

"Good for you. These things will kill you. But I figure, so will everything else that's worth living for, so when it's my time to go, I'll do it with a beer in my hand, a cigarette in my mouth, and a beautiful woman curled up next to me."

"Two out of three ain't bad," Luis, another ranch hand said, coming out of the bunkhouse. He gave a big yawn and scratched his stomach. "Coffee's ready, but I wouldn't get in Bob's way. Something about the soufflé needing to rest."

"I just want scrambled eggs," Frenchie said, closing his eyes.

"And a pound of bacon," Luis said mournfully.

"But Bob had to take a culinary class because he's sweet on the teacher." Frenchie shook his head and flicked his cigarette into the standing ashtray on the side of the porch.

Frenchie and Luis started setting out plates and cutlery at the long picnic tables. Simon pitched in to help and was rewarded with the first cup of coffee. It was dark as mud, but the bitterness was held at bay by notes of chicory and something else he couldn't place. By the time the other retreat center guys got there, he was on his second cup.

They lined up in the kitchen for a slice of the soufflé and scoops of fresh fruit. Simon and the rest of the boys were a little taken aback by the fancy presentation, but they weren't complaining, unlike the ranch hands who were grumbling over it. The tray of sausages and biscuits, however, went fast. Simon was able to snag two of each. It was the best damned food he had ever tasted.

He would have gone back for more, but he was afraid he'd fall off his horse if he did. After breakfast, though, most of the ranch hands went riding out with Nate. The retreat center guys stayed with Esteban, Frenchie and Bob today to do chores around the ranch.

First thing they had to do was muck out the barns. A few of them grumbled, but Simon didn't mind dealing with shit. Especially since the horses were out in a nearby corral and there might be a chance for riding later.

"Are those our horses?" his roommate Chris asked, pointing to a thoroughbred racehorse and a reddish-brown roan.

"Not a chance," Esteban said. "These are the owners' pride and joy. Synergy belongs to Nate's wife, Janice Sullivan. And Pippi over there is Trent Campbell's wife, Kelly Sullivan's horse."

"What about those two?" Chris nodded toward two who were running around the corral.

Esteban snorted. "Not if you're fond of your kneecaps. Ever hear of the wild Grayson sisters?"

"Shit yeah," Chris said.

"That's June's horse Athena, and the one with the leather studded barding is Merry's horse, Raphael. Don't fuck with either of those horses," Esteban warned.

"Isn't June your girl?" Dave, one of the former inmates that Simon hadn't known before the retreat, asked.

"Yeah, stay away from June, too," Esteban said with a grin.

"Does that mean Merry is up for grabs?" Dave asked.

"No," Simon said before he could stop himself.

That caught him a few looks, but he didn't feel the need to explain. When they were done with the stalls, Esteban led them over to the animals that needed food and water. The ranch had chickens, milk cows, and...llamas.

"The llamas are new," Esteban said. "Janice Sullivan's idea. Be lucky you're in the retreat center this year. Next year, knitting is going to be one of the activities. With these guys' wool."

The men snickered.

"I wish I was joking," Esteban said.

Moving on, he showed them the barn where the horses that they were going to be riding were kept.

"You're in charge of feeding, watering, and taking care of these animals." Esteban explained the feeding schedule, and had them bring their horses out to be brushed and showed them how to check their hooves.

Simon was pleased that his teenage years working on various ranches when his father wasn't looking had paid off. The familiar routine came back to him easily and replaced his memories of prison.

He got to ride a horse named Scout who had a docile temperament. Simon supposed that was for the best, but a part of him wanted a horse with a little more spirit.

When Simon and the rest of the men finished up taking care of the horses, Esteban had them saddle up.

"Just like riding a bike," Simon said to Tim, one of the inmates that he had only known by sight when they were in prison.

"I hope I don't get a flat tire," Tim joked.

As they rode down the road, Esteban pointed out some buildings. "That's Trent and Kelly's house. Over there is Trent's rodeo school. They're planning on a charity rodeo the week before Christmas, so you'll see a lot of activity around the ranch as the organizers set up."

All in all, they spent about three hours in the saddle. After they got back from the ride and had taken care of their horses, Esteban called for a fifteen-minute smoke and coffee break. Too much coffee made Simon jittery though, so he headed back out to the paddock where the Sullivan and Grayson horses were.

He enjoyed the mild Texas sun on his face, even as his hands gripped the railing until his knuckles were white. Simon had been fine when he was riding or with the others, but being alone in all the wide-open spaces was starting to get to him. He forced himself to concentrate on the horses instead of the endless open sky. They were all beautiful creatures, the best that money could buy, no doubt.

Scout was a fit-looking animal, but compared to these horses, he was ordinary. These horses were genetically bred to be the masterpieces that they were. Simon hadn't expected to be as horse-struck as a thirteen-year-old girl, but he couldn't stop looking at them. The way they played and frolicked in the paddock eased something in his soul that had been puckered up tight.

Out of the corner of his eye, he saw Charlie Lincoln approaching him. The man had been missing all morning, but then again, he hadn't signed up to be a ranch hand like the rest of them had. Charlie was dressed in faded Levi's and a red-checkered shirt. He blended right in with the ranch hands, if you didn't look too closely. Charlie's eyes were always moving, scanning the area for threats.

Being with Charlie was easy until he started to talk. Because when he started talking, he made Simon think about things he'd rather not deal with.

"How's it going?" Charlie asked.

"So far, so good." Simon hitched his hip against the side

of the corral and turned to face him. "Can't complain. Anything is better than prison."

"Has Esteban been taking it easy on you guys?"

"I hate to think this was easy." Simon's ass was sore and he was getting a blister on his toe from his new boots.

"If you think this is bad, wait until you're out on the range with Nate."

"That's something to look forward to," Simon said dryly. "I don't mind the work. It beats the hell out of my prison job. I was on cleanup duty in the cafeteria." Simon shuddered in memory. He would never eat spaghetti again.

"Well, don't get comfortable working around the ranch. We ease you into horseback riding, but tomorrow you're riding all day and Nate doesn't take kindly to slackers."

"I'm no slacker," Simon said.

"Just let me know if either of the boys work you too hard, though. Sometimes they forget that you guys haven't been on a horse for a long time."

"I expect to be sore," Simon said. "But I am looking forward to spending the day riding around the ranch." Just as long as he wasn't alone. When he was alone, he just wanted to get into his car and pin the gas pedal to the floor.

"It's a little cold for December, but maybe that's the Christmas magic coming out," Charlie said.

Simon snorted. "Christmas magic? Let me guess, you're Santa Claus."

"Just one of his elves."

"Speaking of elves, you wouldn't happen to know any local contractors who specialize in woodworking, electrical, and plumbing, would you?" Simon asked.

"What do you need?"

"My mom's cabin, the one you dropped me off at, needs a lot of work." He thought about what Merry had said about using his father's money to fix up his mother's cabin. While it galled him that he couldn't do it without his help, Braxton owed his dead wife for making her life a living hell. If he told himself he was only doing what his mom would have done if she were alive, it made the thought of using the money easier to swallow.

"What kind of work?"

"The plumbing's shot. Something's been eating the wires. I don't trust some of the floorboards." Simon rubbed the bridge of his nose. "I'm not good at stuff like that. But I'd like to live there when this is all over, at least for a little while. As it is now, I can't."

"I can send a few boys out there and get some estimates for you."

"I'd appreciate that." Simon's body sagged in relief. Charlie was a lifesaver. "I'm not afraid of hard work. I know my way around a hammer and saw. I can help fix it up." He knew he owed his mother for his contributions to her sadness as well. Since he couldn't fix their relationship now, maybe it would be enough that he could fix the cabin she loved so much.

"That would save some money."

Anything that would keep him from using his father's money, when he didn't have to, was all right in Simon's book.

Charlie's eyes got a far-off look as he stared out into the horizon. Following his gaze, Simon saw two men on a Gator all-terrain vehicle. As they got closer, he noticed both of the men had rifles across their laps. Simon felt his prison instincts tighten his shoulder blades.

"Trouble?"

Charlie shook his head. "That's my son, Donnie—Donovan. I think I told you that he runs safaris for the tourists? The rifles are just in case any feral hogs decide to investigate."

"Is that a big problem around here?"

"In the back woods, yes. There's plenty of food and water for them out in the wilderness so they don't have to forage close to the house. But, we still have to be on the lookout for them because they're mean bastards."

Simon expected that Donovan would have slowed down the ATV or at least acknowledged his father with a wave. But he drove on by them, deliberately not looking at Charlie.

That was weird. Still, it was none of his business.

"We don't get along," Charlie said, turning his back on the vehicle.

Simon knew there was a story there, and he equally knew that he didn't want to hear it. Looking down at the dusty ground, he focused the tips of his new boots that were just starting to feel like his instead of something hand-me-down or newly purchased. He was on this ranch because of Charlie. The least he could do was listen to the story that the man obviously wanted to tell.

Or did he? Simon wasn't good with nonverbal clues.

Charlie was frowning at the horses, but Simon didn't think they were the source of his consternation. Maybe Charlie would let him off the hook and start talking. But when the silence grew too awkward, Simon realized he had to step up his social skills.

"What did you do?"

Charlie winced.

Okay, maybe Simon needed to work on his people skills a little bit more, too. But a father and son not speaking was right up his alley, and Simon just assumed that it was because of something Charlie did.

"A lot of things," Charlie said.

For a moment, Simon thought that was it. He'd asked. Charlie had answered. There was no reason to continue the conversation. That hadn't been so hard. Then Charlie elaborated.

"I wasn't the best father."

"You couldn't have been any worse than mine." Simon hadn't known Charlie long, but he already knew he was nothing like his own father. Braxton Reynolds wouldn't piss on a man if he was on fire. He certainly wouldn't help a bunch of ex-cons rehabilitate into society, even if the ex-con was his own son. Probably especially if his son was the ex-con.

"I wouldn't be too sure about that," Charlie said. "An argument could be made that your father had your best interests at heart."

Simon cut him off with a snort.

"I'm not saying it was a good idea to have you thrown in

prison. Or even a compassionate or caring one."

"It was a real fucked-up one," Simon said flatly. He didn't need to hear this. He had heard it from counselors, social workers, and his father's lawyers for the past ten years.

"That it was. But some could say that in some twisted, perverted corner of his brain, he thought he was doing right by you."

Simon shrugged. Bottom line, he didn't give a shit what had motivated his father to ruin his life. As far as he knew, Braxton had been motivated by money, pussy, and screwing over anyone who didn't look like him or was poorer than he was. That was his father in a nutshell, and when his son didn't want to follow in his footsteps, Braxton Reynolds had been a vindictive prick who had wanted to teach him a lesson.

The only lesson Simon learned from him was that if you were a miserable prick your whole life, you died alone. He was glad that he had been able to help his father learn that lesson.

"I, on the other hand," Charlie said, "did not have my son's best interests at heart. I told you I had been a conman, a grifter. So was my wife, and we made our son that way too."

Simon didn't know what to think about that. So he stayed silent.

"Then one day, the reaper came a-callin'. It was one of those pivotal moments that a man has in life, where he could show the universe who he really is." Charlie turned to look at him. "Apparently I'm a coward, a real chickenshit bastard."

It made Simon uncomfortable to hear the pain in Charlie's voice. "Everybody makes mistakes, man. That's the first thing the social workers told us when we're in the joint."

"There are mistakes, son. And then there's *what the hell was I thinking?* catastrophes."

"What was the catastrophe?" Simon said, fully hooked into Charlie's story.

"I conned the wrong man. One who had a gun and was squirrelly nervous about using it. If he had shot me, it would have been justice, I guess. I certainly deserved to be shot after taking money from old people, and the stupid. I wrongly assumed that he wouldn't shoot a child. So I used my own son as a shield to get out of there."

"Fuck," Simon said. That was some cold-hearted bullshit right there.

"I was wrong."

"He shot your kid?" Simon whirled to look at where Donovan and his client were almost a speck on the horizon. "How old was he?"

Charlie didn't seem to hear his question. "My wife, on the other hand, didn't want to take the risk. She moved too fast for a nervous man with the gun. She put herself in between him and Donnie. The bullet hit her instead of my son."

"What did you do?"

"I ran. I got the fuck out of Dodge and left them there."

"Holy shit." Simon gaped at him.

"It's not an excuse, but I panicked. It never occurred to me that he had killed my wife. We were so used to conning people, I thought the bullet had grazed her. I thought she was acting. I thought she'd milk it for all it was worth, and then meet up at one of our safe houses that I set up if things went to shit. It went to shit all right. She died in the hospital three days later. The wound went septic. There was nothing they could do. My son led the police right to me at the safe house."

"What did you do?"

"I went to jail. I deserved it. At first, I thought I might do a suicide by cop, but I didn't want Donovan to see that. He had already watched one of his parents get shot to death. And even if he hated me, which he does, I didn't want him to have to live with the memory of seeing me shot dead in front of him, too."

"How did you wind up together at the same ranch?"

"Sheer luck. I never stopped keeping track of my son. Even though he had made it abundantly clear that he didn't want anything to do with me."

"Why didn't you honor his wishes?" Simon asked, feeling shades of déjà vu. His father hadn't stopped trying to contact him, but that was because Braxton never gave a damn about anyone's feelings but his own. Charlie seemed different. But was he really?

"You'll understand someday when you're a parent."

Simon shook his head in disgust. "I understand that you wanted forgiveness. And I also understand that you probably didn't deserve it."

"You're right on both counts."

He hadn't expected Charlie to agree with him. "Isn't it

hard to see him every day, knowing that he hates you?"

"No, because at least I get to see him every day. I took his mother away from him. I know there's no forgiveness for that. But that's not going to stop me from watching out for him. He married a good woman—Emily."

"Does she hate you?"

"No, the Sullivan sisters have been good to me. They let me be as adjacent to my son as I can be. And who knows? Maybe, there will be grandbabies in my future." Charlie gave a self-depreciating grin. "Anyway, I got to go check on the other guys. You should grab some water. Stay hydrated."

Stay hydrated? That was such a normal thing to say after having dropped a truth bomb on him. Simon was still reeling from Charlie's story and the parallels to Simon's relationship with his own father. Charlie's actions had killed Donovan's mother. Just like Simon's father's actions had killed Simon's mother. And mirroring Braxton Reynolds's manipulations, Charlie had manipulated his way into his son's life, just like Simon's father had tried to manipulate his way into Simon's. He wanted to hate Charlie for that. He wanted to paint Charlie with the same brush that he'd painted his father with: dark and evil. It confused him that he didn't feel that way at all.

Instead, Simon felt sorry for an old man who'd fucked up so bad, that he had to run a grift in order to be close to the only family he had left. Of course, the difference between Charlie and Braxton was that Charlie had paid for his sins. Charlie had spent the majority of his adult life in prison and had been rehabilitated back into society and then decided to help other people.

In the beginning, all Simon had wanted to hear from his father were the words *I'm sorry*. They never came. Then, after a while, even if Braxton had apologized, it wouldn't have made a damn bit of difference. If his father were alive now, Simon wouldn't have anything to do with him. And if his father had shown up on the ranch that he was working at, Simon would have walked away, even if it meant being sent back to jail. A part of him realized that he was still letting the old man manipulate him. That was something he was going to have to work on, but for right now, he knew what he had to do.

Instead of hydrating like Charlie suggested, Simon headed back to the retreat center. Under his bed in a locked box was the letter his father had made sure was included with the legal paperwork that gave Simon the deed to the house and the title of the car. The lawyer said that his father's last wish was for Simon to read the letter. It was a thick one. Simon wondered how many pages someone needed to say they were sorry. But it didn't matter. He wasn't going to let his father get the last word. And while Charlie Lincoln still could try to make amends to his son for getting his mother killed, any such absolution was beyond Braxton Reynolds.

After pocketing the letter and relocking the box, Simon hid it back under the bed. Then he went outside, searching until he found Frenchie, who was smoking another cigarette.

"Got a light?" Simon asked him.

Frenchie handed him a lighter. "I thought you didn't smoke?"

"I don't. I just have some business to finalize." Simon stood over the tall ashtray and lit the letter on fire. He watched as the orange flames licked up the paper. When they got near to his fingers, Simon dropped it on the dusty ground and ground the fire out with his new boot heel. Then he scooped up the embers and tossed them into the bottom of the ashtray.

So much for Braxton Reynolds's last words.

Chapter Seven

MERRY SLEPT IN late, glad for the soft bed, and that she'd had the foresight to extend her payment to the Three Sisters Ranch for another week of taking care of Raphael. Both she and her horse needed some pampering, and she knew that Janice and Emily would make sure Raphael got tip-top care. She dozed in and out throughout the lazy Monday morning, trying not to think about what she needed to do to prepare for the charity rodeo.

Merry would have been in holiday mode, ready to celebrate her birthday and Christmas, if it wasn't for the fact that she was worried LeAnn was going to wipe the floor with her in the bronc-riding event. Merry had to be honest with herself. She wasn't having fun anymore. The rodeo circuit life was getting old, and she hated bronc busting. Part of her just wanted to quit. But that was the coward part of her. And she wasn't a coward. Besides, it was the only belt that she didn't have from the WPRC and she was damned if she was going to retire without having a buckle from every event they offered women riders.

When she and June began on the circuit, the only rodeo event for women had been barrel racing and they had been really good at it. When it expanded to roping, she and her sister had excelled in that as well. While Merry knew it was getting to be time for her to stop making her living on the rodeo circuit, she wondered what the hell else was she going to do.

When her career started taking off, she'd thought she would have to be dragged away from the circuit, kicking and screaming. But lately, it had been an effort to pull on her boots and saddle up. Sure, she still enjoyed the parties and the adrenaline that coursed through her when she rode out to a cheering crowd. However, ever since she took up bronc busting, everything hurt—even when she hadn't been thrown off. Merry didn't want to permanently harm her body. She was going to need it for the next sixty or so years.

Of course, that left the question as to what came next. Was she the type to settle down and get married? A vision of her and Simon walking down the aisle brought a ridiculous thump to her heart. It made her feel like a teenager again. Then, she realized she was putting the cart way before the horse.

She should have taken that announcer job last year.

"Too late now," she told herself. No sense wallowing in regret. Something would come up. It always did. Right now, she had to just manage to stay on the stupid bronc longer than the competition did. But that was easier said than done.

When her phone rang and she saw it was June, she almost didn't answer it. But depending on what June wanted, her next step would be to bang on her door. And Merry definitely didn't want that.

"You're up early," Merry said, throwing an elbow over her eyes.

"Early? It's past ten in the morning," June said, sounding annoyingly awake.

"So?"

"So you better get your ass down here. We're practicing for the charity rodeo today."

That was news to Merry. "Since when?"

June lowered her voice. "Since LeAnn and her family rolled into your B&B last night."

"What?" Merry flung back the covers and leapt to the window, ignoring the protest her back and legs made. Peering through the slats of the window shade, she saw an empty horse trailer with LeAnn's branding on it, as well as the ginormous Winnebago that her family traveled around in. What the hell did they need a room at a bed-and-breakfast for when they could stay in that thing?

"Damn it," she groaned, hoping that they had already eaten breakfast. It would be super awkward to see all of them in the dining area, looking all chipper and perfect.

Merry decided that she didn't need a shower since she'd had one last night after leaving Simon. She was going to get all sweaty anyway practicing, so she pulled on the jeans she'd kicked off last night, shrugged into a T-shirt, and put on a button-down shirt over it. After grabbing her keys, phone, and purse, she hurried out of the room. She figured she would grab a couple of kolaches and a big old cup of coffee on her way out. That would keep her until lunchtime. Putting her hat on her head, she tipped the brim down low to hide her face and headed into the dining room.

But luck wasn't with Merry that day. The entire Keller family was seated around a table. They had a carafe of orange juice, a pot of coffee, and family-style platters of bacon, eggs, and sausage. Merry's stomach growled at the sight, but she prayed that they didn't notice her.

"Merry Grayson? Is that you?" LeAnn called.

Merry's first reaction was to ignore the voice, but then she realized she was being rude. LeAnn Keller was the nicest thing you could ever run across. And Merry wasn't a bitch without good reason. Forcing a smile, she turned and waved.

"Why don't you join us?" LeAnn asked.

"Oh, I couldn't," Merry said, backing away toward the buffet. "I need to get over to the Three Sisters Ranch. June was looking for me."

"We'd love for you to join us," one of LeAnn's sisters said. Merry couldn't remember what her name was, but she did know they were all named after country-western singers.

"I don't want to intrude," Merry said weakly.

"Not at all," her father said. "We'd be honored to have you join us."

LeAnn's mom nodded enthusiastically. "We're big fans."

Well, shit. Merry couldn't find a decent way to get out of this, so she sat down. Besides, out of the corner of her eye, she saw the buffet was all out of kolaches.

"How was your trip?" Merry asked.

"It was great being home for a few days to catch up on things," LeAnn said. "My sister Loretta watches over our home in Dallas while we're on the road. But when we got the call from Trent Campbell, we knew we had to cut our stay short and come out."

"That was very nice of you."

"It's good to get in some extra practice too," LeAnn said. *Like she needed it.*

Merry helped herself to a scoop of scrambled eggs when they passed her the platter. She also accepted bacon, sausage, and some whole-wheat toast—because she was trying to eat healthy. Merry stuffed her face as politely as she could so she didn't have to make conversation. Listening to the family's chatter, she learned LeAnn's two sisters were Dolly and Reba. Reba was a veterinarian and Dolly worked in public relations. Their parents were retired, but her mother had been a barrel racer as a girl and was really into rodeo. In addition to helping Reba with the horses, their father was a mechanic, just like Merry's father had been.

"I bet that comes in handy when the Winnebago breaks down," Merry said.

Mr. Keller rapped his knuckles on the table. "Knock on wood, that hasn't happened yet. But I'm confident that if we do break down, I can get us back on the road."

Merry was tempted to ask him to take a look at her truck. It had started making some funny rattling noises, and she couldn't afford to get it fixed. If she knew where her own dad was, she would have asked him to help, but she hadn't heard from him in a couple years. Although, it was about time that he circled back into their lives. Every couple years or so, he sought her out at a rodeo to say hi, maybe score some free tickets, or get bragging rights that Merry was his daughter. Sometimes, he even included June, which instead of pissing June off, pleased her to no end.

Merry wondered what it would have been like to have a father like Mr. Keller. She would have probably chafed at all the rules, because Mr. Keller looked like he was a rules guy. But on the other hand, they seemed like a nice, happy family. Not that the Graysons weren't a nice, happy family. But as April liked to say, they put the fun in dysfunctional.

"So what made you decide to ride broncos?" Mrs. Keller asked.

"Because they haven't opened up bull riding for women yet," Merry joked.

"Do you think they will?" LeAnn said, leaning forward eagerly.

Mrs. Keller blanched. "No. I don't think they will."

Merry hid a grin behind another spoonful of creamy eggs. If she didn't slow down, she was going to have a stomachache and risk barfing all over the place on her ride.

"What made you get into bronc riding?" Merry asked LeAnn.

"I love it," she said. "I love the feel of the horse, trying to master the wildness. It's like the greatest roller coaster on earth." LeAnn's face lit up when she talked about riding.

Merry admired her passion. She was sorry that she'd never felt that way about bronc riding. It was a chore. A means to an end. Maybe that was why she was so bad at it. Talking with LeAnn made her feel a bit guilty that she resented her so much. It was jealousy, plain and simple. Still, she was happy that LeAnn and the women her age had choices and experiences that Merry and June never had.

Merry was still going to beat her ass in bronc busting, or at least give it her best shot.

"You have another sister, one who doesn't ride, don't you?" Dolly asked.

"Yes, April's an accountant."

Dolly smiled broadly. "I was wondering if the three of you would like to give me an interview for *Cowgirl Today*?"

Merry shrugged. "Sure, but we're not really all that interesting." She was a little taken back by the polite laughter around the table.

"You're a lot more interesting than me," LeAnn said, making a face. "They call me Miss Goody Two-Shoes."

That was probably the nicest thing some of the bitches on the circuit called her. Merry had heard LeAnn referred to as the Virgin Princess and Cocktease Keller, but she wasn't about to say that in front of LeAnn's family. After a quick glance at Dolly, Merry was pretty sure she was aware of what they called her sister. Hopefully, Dolly was good at her job and was keeping that out of the magazines and social media.

"That could be another article," LeAnn's other sister, Reba, said. "*The Angel and the Devil of the Rodeo*." Reba cast her hand in front of her, as if she was looking at a movie marquee.

"Reba, that's rude," her father said.

"I've been called worse," Merry said, smiling at Reba so she knew that she didn't take any offense.

"Not at the breakfast table," her father said.

"Don't be so sure," Merry muttered. June could be particularly territorial about her waffles.

Mr. Keller gave Reba a significant look.

"I'm sorry," Reba said. "I didn't mean anything by it."

"I know. It's all right." Merry nibbled on a slice of bacon.

Sitting down with the Kellers hadn't been the agony she'd been expecting. In fact, it made her miss sitting down for a family meal. She should probably do that soon. Maybe she'd see if her mother had mellowed about Simon after all these years. She could bring him over for Sunday dinner. But first, she'd had to check and see if the retreat schedule allowed him that time. When they had been dating, she had been too embarrassed about living in a trailer to consider bringing him over for dinner. It had been obvious that he came from money, even when he wasn't going for joyrides in the Corvette.

Merry's phone rang. It was June. "Excuse me, I gotta get this." She took the last triangle of toast and got up from the table. "What?"

"Are you still in bed?"

"No, I stopped for breakfast."

"Well, someone's pretty confident that they don't need any extra practice," June said waspishly.

"Who pissed in your Post Toasties this morning?"

"I didn't have any Post Toasties. Some of us are in a bed-and-breakfast. Some of us are just in a bed."

"Last I checked, there were plenty restaurants where you could grab breakfast," Merry said. "And I know Mama keeps a box of Frosted Flakes in the house just for you."

"I didn't have the time or the money to spare this morning."

"I'll see what I can grab you from the buffet," Merry said.

"Just as long as you don't forget the coffee." June hung up.

"Unbelievable." Merry shook her head. Cruising over to the buffet table, Merry filled a Styrofoam container with pancakes and sausages. She didn't bother with the syrup because it would just get all over the place. She added a banana on top, just in case June also wanted to eat healthy. Closing it up, she filled up two coffee to-go mugs, making the coffee sweet and light just the way she and her sister liked.

After paying the cashier for the extra breakfast and coffees, she went back to the Kellers' table. "I've got to get going. June wants breakfast." She held up the to-go container. "It was nice talking with you. Thank you for the food and company." Swallowing her pride, Merry looked at LeAnn. "Good luck in the bronc-riding event. But not too much luck." Merry gave her a genuine smile and headed out to the ranch.

She found herself humming Christmas carols before she could stop herself. Last Stand wasn't Tahiti, but Merry would make the best of it. She was looking forward to doing all the traditional Last Stand things, and dragging Simon around town, doing the things they used to do when they were kids.

But first, the bronc.

Chapter Eight

A FTER JUNE WOLFED down her breakfast, they went a few turns around the barrels with Raphael and Athena, and got to practice their team calf roping before the other candidates trickled in. Word of mouth traveled fast in Last Stand and it looked like everyone wanted to get in some practice for the rodeo.

While Merry was waiting her turn in the bronc-riding pen, she watched the other riders with a jaundiced eye. There were good, and looked comfortable on the greens. They also recovered faster than she could, even after Merry had swallowed a few painkillers to ease the soreness in her muscles. Depressed and a little dejected, Merry turned her attention to something more pleasant—like the wonderful night that she and Simon had just had.

Simon had been everything she had remembered, and yet the boy she knew was no longer there. But that was all right—she wasn't the same girl she'd been back then either. Unfortunately, she didn't know if they had a future or if this was just one hell of a good time.

It felt weird to be dating her high school boyfriend. It felt weird to be dating, period. She had learned a long time ago that it was best to have a good time and then go your separate ways before any feelings could get involved. Unfortunately, it was too late for her. She'd never stopped having feelings for Simon.

"You couldn't pay me to get on a horse like that," her sister April said, climbing up on the rail alongside her.

"Good. Less competition for me." April was terrified of horses, although lately, she had been a lot less skittish around them. They had Cole Lockwood to thank for that. He was a trainer at Trent Campbell's rodeo school. He was also April's fiancé.

"Looks like Keller is the one to beat."

"Tell me about it," Merry groused.

"Just don't get too upset when you lose the barrel-racing competition to me. Again," June said, joining them by hoisting herself up on the railing as well.

Merry resisted the urge to push her sister off and into the pile of horse shit below them. "I don't get upset. I get even."

"Keep it up, and you'll get coal in your stocking. Santa knows if you've been naughty or nice," April said.

"The nice train left the station a long time ago. For both of us," Merry said, gesturing to herself and June.

"You got that right," April agreed. "What do you think we should get Mom for Christmas?"

"Something expensive." Their mother had what she called champagne tastes on a beer budget. If they all pulled their money together, they could get her something special for the holiday.

"Perfume?" June suggested.

"Maybe a new purse?" Merry crossed her arms and scowled at the sun. "It doesn't even feel like Christmas."

"What are you complaining about?" April asked.

"Christmas should be spent on the beach, surrounded by men in Speedos and an unlimited bar tab." Merry still hadn't gotten over the hurt of being left behind. Zane and Carly were probably partying it up in Tahiti while she was here, looking to get on another bronc. They had abandoned her without a second glance. She'd gone from being so mad about it she could spit, to wanting to cry into Raphael's mane. It must be that time of the year because she usually wasn't so emotional. Maybe it was seeing Simon again that was dredging up all the feelings she usually kept tucked under her saddle.

"I don't think it's warm enough for Speedos," April said.

"Exactly," Merry sighed.

"Have you heard from Luke?" June asked.

Merry shook her head. "Nope. Mama hasn't heard from him either."

"He'll be here," April said. "He usually shows up around your birthday."

"Sometimes he does," Merry said, remembering a few times when she'd only got a phone call or a card.

"I can't wait to introduce him to Esteban," June said.

"And Cole," April added.

If she hadn't been so worried about her mother's reaction to her dating Simon again, maybe she would have been excited about reintroducing Simon to Luke. She wasn't sure if Luke would remember her high school boyfriend or not.

Luke had pretty much been gone for those years.

"Getting laid regularly has really affected your brains," Merry said sourly.

"You should try it sometime," June said.

"I'm working on it," Merry said.

June whooped, drawing attention to them. Merry glared at anyone who gave them the stink-eye for being rowdy. They were outside at a rodeo practice, not inside church or playing golf.

"Already?" June crowed. "You work fast. Anyone I know?"

Merry didn't like to lie to her sister, or to anyone really. But the last thing she needed was to have June and April harp on her about hooking up with Simon Reynolds again.

"It's still new." And it was. One night didn't mean anything. How many times had she thought things were going great only to be ghosted the next morning? Too many times. She made a face.

"When do we get to meet him?" April asked.

"How about never?"

"Don't be like that," June wheedled.

"If it goes anywhere, I'll bring him around." Merry hoped it did, but she didn't want to open that can of worms right now—not until she was able to ease her mother into the idea.

She had to remind herself that Simon wasn't here for her, though. He was at the ranch to get his own head on straight. The last thing he needed was pressure when they had decided to keep things fun. However, holidays might just be bearable if he was there enduring them with her.

"Invite him to Christmas dinner," June said.

"There's not enough room for all of us as it is. We don't need one more," Merry said, just to see how far June was willing to push for it.

"There's always room for one more, especially around Christmas," April said.

"We'll see," Merry said, hopping down from the fence and avoiding the horse shit. It was almost her turn to ride.

April followed her back to where they were setting up Merry's bronc, Tweety Pie. Someone at the Double Three Ranch where she had bought the horse from, had a peculiar sense of humor when it came to naming the horses. Tweety Pie was an ornery son of a bitch who liked to kick, bite, and stomp on anything that got in his way. He had cost a fortune, and Merry would have to win in February to pay down her credit card bill. But she had needed a horse like him to practice on when she wasn't at an event.

"Guess who's going to be Santa Claus?" April asked, touching the wall and smoothing down one of the posters that advertised the Christmas rodeo.

"Esteban?" Merry said, naming June's boyfriend.

"Better. Janice convinced Nate to do it."

"I've only met the man a few times, but he doesn't seem to have the temperament that one would expect from Santa Claus."

"You'd be surprised what the love of a good woman would do to a fella."

"Love makes everybody crazy. Just look at Mama."

Their mother went through men like she did shoes. Merry wasn't sure who the latest one was. It was probably still her landlord at the trailer park, since he was the only one who had been hanging around.

Merry was not looking forward to the Christmas lovefest between her mother and her beau du jour, April and Cole, and June and Esteban. She needed to convince Simon to go to Christmas dinner, even if it would go over like a fart in church once her mother found out. For the first time, they would all have boyfriends at the same time.

It was something to think about, but she couldn't allow herself to be distracted at the moment. Tweety Pie was trying to slam his way out of the chute.

"Are you ready?" one of the rodeo volunteers asked her.

"Let's do this."

Merry settled herself onto Tweety Pie, who absolutely hated having her there. She wrapped the rope around her hand, then gave the nod. The gate opened and Tweety Pie took off in an impressive show of rage. She held on as best she could, waving the arm she wasn't holding the rope with as high as she could. If she touched Tweety Pie with it, she'd lose. Tightening her thighs around his girth, Merry still bounced out of the saddle hard, and felt herself about to be thrown.

Shit. Shit. Shit. Thud.

Instinct had her rolling to the side and the bullfighters who had volunteered to help with the broncs hoisted her up and over the railing before Tweety Pie could wheel back around on her. The pick-up riders moved in to flank Tweety

Pie and calm him down.

Dusting off the seat of her pants, Merry scowled at the horse who was now docilely trotting back to the pen in between the other two horses.

"I think you'd have a better time riding a bull," June said.

"Some days, it feels like that." Merry absently rubbed her rib that was still sore from the knock she'd taken back in Argentina.

She needed to get better at this. Keller was graceful where Merry was awkward. Keller mastered the horse where she was hanging on for dear life. Merry felt as unsure as a new colt, and she knew that it showed. She hated not being the best.

"You've had a hell of a career," June started to say.

Merry cut her off. "It ain't over yet." Not until she won that bronc-busting belt next year.

Shrugging, June said, "Just who are you trying to impress?"

"No one," Merry scoffed, and tried not to limp as she circled around to the volunteers. "Let's put Tweety Pie back in rotation and set up for another run," she said.

"You got it," one of the volunteers said.

"Then what are you trying to prove?" June said. "I'm worried about you. You could get seriously hurt."

"I know what I'm doing," Merry said, and stopped rubbing her ribs when June's eyes focused on them.

"I know you do," June said. "But it doesn't look like you're having fun anymore. This was supposed to be about having a good time while making money. You're not doing either."

Merry wanted to hit something, preferably her sister. But she never swung first so she just gritted her teeth and stalked away. She went over to the next paddock where Raphael and Athena were grazing.

"Merry! Merry!"

Still scowling, Merry whirled to see who was calling her name. It was a young girl, maybe about seven or eight years old. Stopping dead in her tracks, Merry forced a pleasant expression. She crouched down, even though her thighs were screaming at her for doing it.

"Hey, what can I do for you?"

"I love to watch you ride," the little girl said. "I'm Dina."

This was the best part of doing rodeo. It made up for not earning a lot of money and getting tossed off a horse.

"Thank you. Do you ride?"

"I'm one of June's students. My uncle is Esteban." June was teaching barrel racing part-time at Trent's school while she waited for the new rodeo season to start.

"June's a good teacher. Nice to meet you, Dina." She held out her hand and they shook.

"June says she's going to beat you at barrel racing."

"June likes to run her mouth."

Dina giggled. "Do you think you're going to win?"

Merry looked over to where June was talking with one of the rodeo volunteers and gave her a grim smile. "Count on it." She might not be able to beat LeAnn Keller, but she sure as hell could leave her sister in the dust.

MERRY PRACTICED A bunch more times on Tweety Pie. She fell off, got slammed into the side of the fence, and narrowly avoided getting nipped in the arm by that ornery horse. She was never so glad as to swap him out with Raphael for barrel racing. Raphael and Tweety Pie were like day and night. Merry and Raphael had been working together for a long time, and it was probably getting to the time where she would have to think about retiring her horse from active competition. And like Merry getting out of rodeo, it should happen sooner rather than later.

"We got one more season in us, don't we, Raphael?" Merry wasn't sure what was going to happen at the end of the season if they didn't come up on top.

Merry did much better in the barrel racing time trials than she did in the bronc ones. Raphael lived to fly around the barrels. They beat Keller by a good five seconds and June by a good two and a half seconds. That was still close, but Merry was confident she could win.

When she got through practicing for the day, Merry and June hung around to talk to some of the fans who had stopped by to watch the practice, and to sign autographs. But Merry felt her attention drift and her eyelids droop after about half an hour.

"I'm going to get some rest," Merry said. It had been a long day after a long night.

"Are you going to hook up with your booty call?" June asked.

"No one says that anymore." Merry avoided the question and led Raphael back to the barn. She saw few ranch hands who she didn't recognize from Esteban's crew, and she figured they were part of Charlie Lincoln's retreat.

Nonchalantly, she wandered over where she had no business being, for the sole purpose of looking for Simon. A few of the men recognized her, and she spent some time talking with them before Esteban shooed her away so they could get back to work.

Out of the corner of her eye, she saw Simon come out of one of the barns. He looked as tired as she felt, and he had a good layer of dirt on him. He was one of those men who grimed up real good. She gave him a broad smile, but was taken aback when he not only didn't return it, but turned and walked away from her without even saying hello.

What the serious hell was that all about?

She had her pride, so she didn't call out or chase him down. If that was the way he wanted to treat her, fine. She had thought they were going to be dating, but somehow between dinner last night and five o'clock this afternoon, Simon must've decided to keep it as a one-night stand.

Figures.

Merry was disappointed and more than a little hurt. But fuck him. That was just the way these things went sometimes. Blinking back tears, she thought, "Well, that didn't take long."

Chapter Nine

SIMON WAITED TILL after dinner and they were given free time before calling Merry. He got into his car and drove into the center of Last Stand, hoping that she was in the mood to get some peach pie at the Draeger Peach Haus in town. He was still hungry, even though he had polished off his share of the steak tips and noodles at the ranch house for dinner with the hands. Besides, there was always room for pie.

Merry didn't answer the phone the first time he called, and Simon didn't bother to leave a message. Maybe she was doing rodeo stuff or was busy with her family. He waited about half an hour, just wandering up and down Main Street seeing the Christmas decorations and the advertisement for the Christkindlmarkt this weekend. There were barrels set out on the street corners, looking for donations for the annual toy drive. He'd have to stop by a toy store and see what he could find. He tried Merry again.

This time he left a message on her voicemail. "Hey, I'm standing outside of Draeger Peach Haus. You want to get some? Pie that is."

Before he could put it back into his pocket, it rang. It

was Merry.

"Hey, gorgeous," he drawled.

"What the fuck is going on with you?" she asked. "You acted like I didn't exist earlier."

Ouch. Yeah, he had. He had hoped she had understood what he had been doing. He guessed he'd been wrong.

"Hey, I'm sorry about that," he said. "I just didn't want the other guys at the retreat to know you and I were dating."

"Why the fuck not? Are you embarrassed by me?" Her voice crackled angrily on the other end of the line.

"No. Why would you even think that? Any man would be proud to have you by their side—myself included. I'm the ex-con. You're the golden girl of the rodeo."

Merry snorted. "You got me mistaken for LeAnn Keller. I've never been golden. I may not wear a Stetson that says *Bad Reputation* like June does, but that's only because I don't need to advertise mine."

"Well, I don't want my bad reputation to tarnish your bad reputation."

"Don't be an idiot," she said.

Simon hated the fact that his good intentions had hurt Merry. "Look, let me make it up to you. I've been craving some of Draeger's peach pie."

"Aren't you afraid to be seen with me?" Merry asked tartly.

"No one in town knows who I am. It's been too long. I was afraid that the retreat guys would be the match that started the gossip fire. Everyone there admires you and your sister. It would have been too juicy of a secret to keep that you were dating an ex-con."

"I told you that I don't care about all of that."

"And I told you that I do."

She sighed. "You're lucky that the Peach Haus has really awesome food, and my mother made cabbage rolls for dinner. I was going to get takeout anyway. The bed-and-breakfast I'm staying at only serves breakfast, so I'm on my own for most of my meals. It's been getting a little expensive eating out, so you're paying, Mr. Moneybags."

"It's a deal." Simon was glad to take Merry out on a real date. "I'll get us a table. Meet me inside."

"See you soon," she said.

While he waited for her, Simon got a table in the back of the restaurant, just in case anyone did recognize him. It was a long shot, but he had gone to Last Stand high school with Merry for a few years. However, in the months leading up to his parents' divorce, his attendance had been shoddy at best. His father had enrolled him into a snooty private school closer to his ultra-fine bachelor pad, but Simon had cut school more often than not while he was there, as well. That along with the fact that Simon had been gone for ten years, he didn't expect anyone to come over and talk with him about the good old days.

Surprisingly enough, he did recognize a few faces, mostly members of Last Stand's founding families. He saw Jasper Corbyn, the owner of People's Bank of Last Stand, and Shane Highwater, the police chief, as they picked up to-go orders. Simon scrunched down in his seat and held his menu up over his face until the chief was gone. Highwater hadn't been in that position ten years ago and probably wouldn't have remembered him anyway, but Simon didn't want to take any chances.

"What can I get you?" the waitress asked.

Going from memory of what Merry liked, Simon ordered two large lemonades and an order of stuffed mushrooms for an appetizer. Once Merry got there, she could pick out what she wanted for dinner. He already had a meal of pork chops at the retreat, but he would order something so Merry didn't feel self-conscious eating all by herself.

When Merry walked in a few minutes later, she was greeted by just about everyone. So much for keeping a low profile. He only hoped that the camera phones would concentrate on her, instead of on him. Simon didn't need the internet sleuths digging up dirt. Although having been imprisoned for the last ten years, he didn't have any social media accounts, so his digital footprint was almost nil. Still, it only took one obsessed fan with a lot of time on their hands to publicly link the two of them together.

Standing up as she came closer to the table, he gave her a kiss on the cheek and was happy to see that she blushed. He'd made Merry Grayson blush. He didn't think that was possible.

"How was your day?" he asked as she sat down. "Are you limping a bit?"

"My ass hurts," she said.

"Want me to kiss it better?"

"You've got to buy me dinner first," she joked.

"What looks good to you?" he asked, sliding over the laminated menu.

"You do, cowboy. And you smell good, too." Merry sniffed in his direction in appreciation.

"I think that's the peach pie you're smelling."

"Do you have some of that on your neck? I'll have to lick you there to see if you taste as good as you smell."

Yes, please.

"If I didn't think it would be sticky as hell," Simon said, "I'd slather the pie somewhere else you could lick."

When Merry smiled, it did things to him. It made him feel goofy. It made him feel like a dumb eighteen-year-old kid who wanted to show off for a pretty girl. The only problem was, he didn't have anything to show off with. Not anymore. At least he still had the car.

When the waitress came back with the stuffed mushrooms, she took their order. Merry decided on the roast beef meal complete with candied carrots and mashed potatoes and gravy. It sounded so good, Simon ordered one for himself, too.

"I'm so happy I don't have to worry about calories," Merry said. "At least, not this week. I can't believe Trent and his crew are throwing this all together on such short notice."

"How are ticket sales?" he asked.

"I'm not sure. I'll ask Janice the next time I see her. We might have to do some promotions, either on the local radio stations or at a booth at the Christmas market. Speaking of which, do you want to go with me to the market this weekend?"

"As long as you're sure you don't mind being seen with me."

"Knock that shit off." She threw a roll from the bread basket at him.

"As long as you're sure that being with me, being seen with me," he corrected himself, "wouldn't cause you problems at your job."

"The only thing causing the problems at my job right now, is a horse named Tweety Pie."

"Sweetie pie?"

She barked out a sharp laugh. "Yeah, not even close. He's from the same ranch that raised Tinkerbell. Stinkerbell is more like it. I didn't buy that horse. I just rode him for the competitions in Argentina. Well, I guess it's more accurate to say that I tried to ride him. I spent more time on my ass than I did in the saddle. I bought Tweety Pie hoping to get some practice in before the U.S. season started up again."

"I admire you," he said, buttering the roll she had tossed at him. "It's not an easy thing to compete in a sport that's brand new to you."

"You don't have to butter me up like that roll," Merry said. "I'm already going to sleep with you tonight. I don't care how sore my muscle are."

"Too bad the retreat is full of horny men. We could've soaked in Janice's hot tub."

"Isn't there a hot tub at your place? I seem to remember one…" Merry gave him such a lascivious grin, he immediately got hard. Maybe they could get their order to go. No, she deserved a fun night out. They didn't have to spend all their time in the bedroom, though they'd get there eventually. Besides, the last thing he wanted to do was go back to his father's house, even if Merry would be there with him.

"I'll go with you to the Christmas market on Saturday as long as it fits in with the retreat's schedule," he said.

"Why don't we go at night? It's prettier then anyway, with all the colorful lights." Merry leaned back as the waitress brought out two large plates.

"I missed this," he admitted as they dug in.

"I missed you," she said with her mouth full. "You should have called me when you got out of prison the first time."

"It was for the best," he said, trying not to let the regret he felt spoil his appetite.

"Just as long as you know that I don't need you to be my white knight anymore. I accept you for who you are, and I don't care who knows it. Except maybe my mother," she added, almost as an afterthought. "She still thinks you're the devil."

"Sorry about that. I don't want to cause any friction between the two of you."

"There's always friction between us. Don't worry, she'll come around once she sees how awesome you are."

"I don't know about that." Now it was his turn to blush. He concentrated on the hearty food in front of him and hoped she wouldn't notice.

Merry took a long drink of her lemonade. "Can I tell you something that I haven't told anyone, not even my sisters?"

"You can tell me anything," he said.

"I've been thinking about retiring for about a year now. I had a rodeo announcer's job all lined up, but in the end, I turned it down. Things came up with June last year and I decided to delay my retirement. Then when the WPRC added bronc busting as a new event for women, I knew I had to win a buckle in that before I left."

"Well, I know you can do anything that you put your mind to."

"I've got some issues. And I hate riding broncs. So I'm not sure how these next couple of years are going to work out. And they gave the announcer job to someone else."

"There will be other jobs," he said, reaching across the table to hold her hand.

It was nice having dinner with her. He wanted something normal in his life again. They had gone out on dates like this when they were in high school. They'd go for dinner and a movie. Or go horseback riding in the moonlight on state park trails with horses he'd bribed the ranch hands at his job into letting them use.

"So, is the retreat center doing anything for you guys during the holidays?" she asked after they ordered dessert—peach pie a la mode. He was going to be stuffed, but he didn't care.

"They're going to have a Christmas Eve dinner for everyone. Then, we have Christmas Day off. But a lot of the guys don't have any family nearby, so Janice is having lunch catered in the dining room that day. The ranch hands are going to join us, and there's a secret Santa." He rolled his eyes.

"Have you guys picked names yet?"

"Yeah, I got Frenchie."

"What are you going to get him?"

"A carton of cigarettes and a six-pack of Budweiser."

Merry pretended to wipe a tear from the corner of her eye. "How sentimental."

"It's a gift I know he'll use and enjoy. What would you get him?"

"I don't know. A striptease and a bullwhip."

Simon blinked at her in surprise as heat and jealousy reared up in him. "You got a thing for Frenchie I should know about?"

"No, I just know cowboys."

"Well, I'm not giving him a striptease."

"How about giving me one?" she asked, running the toe of her boot up his calf.

"All you had to do was ask." Simon signaled the waitress. "Check please."

AFTER DINNER, MERRY was surprised that Simon didn't drive them back to his father's house for a rowdy and raunchy round two. Instead, he found a drive-in theater a few towns over that was showing Christmas movies from the early 2000s.

She couldn't believe that Simon would sit through a drive-in edition of *Love Actually*, but she supposed enough buttered popcorn and large, crisp sodas made everything more bearable. Truthfully, she would've watched a blank screen just for the experience of sitting next to him in the gorgeous Corvette.

"I thought we were going to head back to your place," she said.

"Next time." He leaned over and kissed her, jostling the popcorn bucket between them.

"Aren't you worried about getting butter stains on the leather seats?" Merry loved this car and couldn't figure out why he wasn't a clean freak about it like some of the men she knew were about their cars.

"If we do, it can be cleaned. And if it can't—" He shrugged. "It's a memory. A good memory." Reaching over, he squeezed her hand.

Merry liked the idea of collecting memories like they were stocking stuffers that she could pull out and admire. She linked her fingers through his and they held hands while watching the movie. It was easy to get into the Christmas spirit watching all the beautiful people up on the wide screen. Maybe there was a little kernel of Christmas magic starting to pop in her heart.

Or maybe it was indigestion.

"Next time, we can take my pickup. I've got a camper shell top to put over the bed of the truck."

"In case it gets too cold?"

"No, so we can have sex."

"Have mercy," Simon said.

"I told you, that's not my forte."

Merry should've known that this sweet and sexy date

wouldn't be all sunshine and rainbows. During the intermission after *Love Actually* ended, but before Reese Witherspoon's *Four Christmases* started up, when they were getting refills at the concession stand, a couple of eager fans came up to her and asked for some selfies. She posed with them and talked with them until it was time to go back to their cars. The opening credits hadn't even ended when her phone started blowing up.

April. She ignored it, allowing the call to go to voicemail. Then June. Voicemail.

Finally, her mother. That was definitely a voicemail.

And then it started again.

"Uh-oh," she said, putting her phone on silent.

"What's wrong?"

"My sisters and my mom keep calling."

"Shouldn't you answer them?"

She had a feeling she knew what this was about. She checked social media just to confirm. Yup. Viral. Her and Simon. That had been quick. "I guess the cat is out of the bag." Merry showed him the TikTok one of the fans had filmed of them walking back to Simon's car.

Who is the mystery man in Merry Grayson's life?

"At least they don't know who I am, yet," Simon said.

"They don't. But guess who does?"

They both looked down as her phone flickered.

"I warned you," Simon said.

"And I told you I didn't care. I'll handle my family."

"Can I help?" he asked.

Merry watched the movie screen for a few minutes.

"Yeah, I think you can."

"Anything."

"Do you mean that?"

"I wouldn't have said it, if I didn't."

"Okay then." She turned to him. "I want you to spend Christmas with my family."

"Say what? I thought your mother hated me."

"Hate's a strong word. I can talk her down from that. It's Christmas and my birthday after all. Special things happen for me at this time of year. And, this time, you're part of that something special."

"I don't know," he said.

Now it was Simon's turn to watch the movie. The silence stretched between them so long, Merry went back to her popcorn and concentrated on Vince Vaughn navigating Christmas with his brothers.

"I got a better idea," Simon said, turning toward her.

"I'm all ears."

"Do you remember my mother's cabin?"

"Do I? We spent many hours playing house there. I loved that place. Whatever happened to it?"

"It got neglected. It's mine now, too. It needs a lot of work, but I think I could have it ready in time to host your family for Christmas."

Merry couldn't believe her ears.

"It would be a tight fit."

"Not as tight as my mother's double-wide."

"Do you think it would make me more acceptable to your mom?"

"Shit, yeah. My mother loves a redemption story. Why

do you think she kept taking my father back all those times?"

"Your father?"

"Luke Ford, like the pickup truck. Only he was a pick-up man, if you catch my meaning. Anyway, Luke had always promised my mom that one day we'd all move into a house together, just one big happy family. Well, that never happened and eventually Mama moved on to other men with other false promises."

"Ouch." Simon winced.

"Anyway, if I tell her what really happened, that it was your own house that your father chased you out of, and that he was the one who sent you to prison, she'll switch her attitude to Team Simon faster than you could spit."

"I can spit pretty fast," he said.

"It's not speed that counts. It's distance. But that's neither here nor there. Combine that with you offering your house…"

"It's going to take a lot of work."

"Well, lucky for you, I've got some time on my hands. I'll do whatever it takes to get your mom's cabin Christmas ready."

"First it has to be human ready. But Charlie's contractor friends are looking at it this week."

"I'm so excited about this. You're the best." She threw her arms around him and hugged him tight.

When she went to move back to her own seat, he didn't let her go. Instead, Simon took the opportunity to tug her shirt free from her pants.

"Well, hello cowboy," Merry purred as he deftly unclipped her bra.

Chapter Ten

H E KISSED HER because he couldn't resist her sweet mouth anymore. She tangled her fingers in his hair. It was awkward getting close with the gear shift in between them, but they made do. It was familiar because they had done this before, in this same car. Being at the drive-in was new, but that was all right. As the movie played on around them, Simon concentrated on her supple body. The curves of her breasts, the turgid peaks of her nipples and the smooth, soft skin of her stomach and back. She was perfect.

Simon unbuttoned her jeans and slid his hand into her panties.

"Wait," she said, pushing away from him.

"Sorry." Christ, what was he doing? They weren't kids anymore who had to sneak around. He could take her home and have her all to himself in a big king-size bed.

Tugging off her boots, Merry yanked down her pants and panties and launched herself back at him. "Okay, continue."

Then again, who was he to argue?

He tugged her shirt and bra over her head and enjoyed the sight of a naked woman in his car. In prison, he'd had fantasies like this. Simon had a moment to wonder if anyone could see in, but his windows were tinted and the windshield was pretty fogged up. Then she was kissing him, tearing at his shirt, so buttons went flying. Her little nips on his neck sent a savage thrill through him and he moved his hand back between her legs.

She parted her thighs for him, giving him the access he needed to finger her.

"Yeah," she groaned, swaying her hips against his hand.

After kissing down his chest, Merry unbuttoned his jeans with her teeth. Simon eased the seat back and she slithered on top of him. There wasn't a lot of room in the low-slung car, and Merry banged her knee on his driver's side window as she maneuvered her body to take his cock in her mouth while presenting him with her sweet pussy. But they made it work.

He was licking her from top to bottom when she sucked him deep and hard. Groaning, he wrapped his arms around her hips and plunged his tongue into her. He alternated penetrating her with it, to licking circles around her clit. The noises she was making around his cock were driving him wild, but he was determined to get her off before she made him come. He didn't have long to wait. With each hard suck, he licked her in a frenzied need to taste every inch of her. Merry squirmed, moaned and shook. And when she screamed, it was only partially silenced because he was halfway down her throat.

Simon only had time for a grunt of satisfaction before his eyes rolled back and he tensed. He came with an equal intensity that shook him to the core. She lay on top of him panting and he didn't have the strength to move. He stroked her ass and kissed her thigh, holding her tight.

"Have I mentioned that you're amazing?" he said when he rediscovered how to speak.

"Have I mentioned that I'm stuck?"

"I can help." Gently, he lifted her up his body and eased her into the passenger's side seat.

"I'm dizzy." She laughed. "All the blood went to my head."

He righted the soda they had knocked over in their frenzy. Luckily the cover was on tight. "Drink this." The popcorn hadn't survived. He didn't mind the thought of vacuuming it up. It had been worth it.

She drank most of the soda while she searched around for her clothes. He watched avidly as she did a reverse striptease. Raising his seat back up, he held her bra out to her. "I don't remember doing that when we were dating."

"I blew you plenty of times," she said.

He remembered. "I meant the acrobatics."

"A girl's got to keep her man on her toes," she said with an impish grin.

"I don't deserve you."

Merry scowled. "Please don't start that shit again."

He held up his hands in surrender. "You win. I'm completely under your spell."

"Good," she said, cuddling back into him. As they watched the rest of the movie, he stroked her hair and tried not to think about the shit-show his Christmases had been.

But with all the dysfunction on the screen with the holiday parties, he couldn't help it.

He had only spent one Christmas vacation at his father's house. His mother had been in the hospital after falling down the stairs while she was drunk. His father had spent most of the week "on business," which Simon knew meant he was banging his new secretary. That left him alone with his step-monster Joyce.

Joyce, who had only been a few years older than he was, wanted to have a special Christmas too. She had lit the fire and arranged for a nice romantic steak and lobster dinner for two. The candlelight and soft music should have clued him in. But he had been too busy devouring his dinner and trying to come up with a way to get to Merry that night. But his father had the car and the only other choice was to convince Joyce to give him her keys.

Unfortunately, having him leave had not been part of her plans for the night.

She had been dressed in a ridiculous little red velvet dress with a white fur trim. She complained about being too hot in it, and at the time, Simon could understand why. The fire was roaring. It was sixty degrees out and she was wearing velvet.

However, he hadn't expected her to take it off at the table. Or that she would be wearing a red lace bra and panties set underneath. He'd nearly choked on his lobster in shock. And then when she knelt by his chair, Simon had bolted to his feet.

He didn't remember what he said, just recalled running

upstairs to his room and locking his door. It occurred to him many years later that if he had really wanted to get even with his father, he should have fucked Joyce on their dining room table on Christmas Eve.

Instead, he had put on headphones and tried to forget what had happened. After that, he made it a point never to be alone with Joyce again. She never mentioned the situation either, but the next year, she had been out with someone else when his dad had come home and caught him and Merry.

Maybe his father had suspected he'd find his son banging his wife and that was why he'd come home early, unannounced...and with a gun.

Simon couldn't help wondering if Braxton would have shot him—or Joyce—if that had been the case.

That line of thought brought Charlie Lincoln to mind.

"It's fucked up," he said.

"Hmmm?" Merry said.

Simon realized she had been dozing off.

"Nothing, babe." He kissed the top of her head.

He just hoped he wasn't bringing any bad shit to her doorstep. Trouble had a way of finding him—he wanted to be free and clear of it before he brought anybody else into the mess of his life. And the first thing he had to do was get rid of that house and find another place to live.

Merry gave a cute little snore.

But it would have to wait until after Christmas, because he was a sucker.

THE NEXT DAY, he was moving cattle on the Three Sisters Ranch. Simon loved being out on his horse. Sure, the work was back-breaking, and the December sun was hot on his neck. His shoulders ached and he was getting blisters on his hands. But damn if he didn't feel good. Even if he had done a dumb thing and invited Merry and her family to have Christmas in a cabin that, at the moment, didn't have a working toilet. What the hell did he know about throwing a party anyway? As it was, it was taking all he had to learn how to be a better ranch hand.

"Frenchie, take Simon with you and bring those calves back to the group," Esteban said, gesturing to three strays who were getting too far behind.

He and Frenchie wheeled away from the rest of the riders and galloped toward the wayward cattle.

This was his first week in the saddle and he was exhausted. He didn't think he'd be too tired for sex, but last night, he could barely keep his eyes open after the movies. Thankfully, Merry hadn't seemed to mind as she had slept through the second half of the movie.

Next week, the work rotation would be scattered as each of the retreat guys teamed up with a ranch hand. He hoped he would have to work next Friday so he could have an excuse to get out of going to the annual Last Stand Christmas parade. Friday night, Santa himself would light the big Christmas tree in front of the library. And then Main Street would be closed until Monday for the Christkindlmarkt. He didn't want to face the crowds. He'd much rather be working on the ranch than putting the effort into appearing normal. Although, he needed the practice, if he didn't want to become a hermit or a workaholic.

Meanwhile, the excitement over the charity rodeo the weekend after the Christmas market was all anyone could talk about. The retreat schedule had him and the former inmates working at the Three Sisters Ranch from Monday through Friday that week so they could be free to watch the rodeo on Saturday. Merry was one of the best riders he'd ever seen, but LeAnn was the better bronc buster. Simon wanted to be there for Merry if she lost to the younger woman.

After they got back to the ranch house around dinner-time, Charlie Lincoln was waiting for him.

"My boys took a look but here's their estimate."

Simon took the envelope from Charlie and opened it up. Ten grand. Shit. That was all he had left of his mother's inheritance. But if he split the bill with his father's estate, that might let him keep some money to live on until he got a job. Still, the desire to do this without any help from Braxton Reynolds was strong. What would his mother have wanted?

"When can they start?" Simon asked.

"They're going to need half up front."

"I can pay cash if they can put a rush on it."

Charlie's eyebrows rose. "Cash huh?"

Simon held up a hand to stop Charlie from getting the wrong idea. "I inherited some money. It's perfectly legit. You're welcome to come to the bank with me."

"It's not that I don't trust you," Charlie said.

"No, I get it. The next day off I have, we'll go."

"I'll let the boys know," Charlie said, and they shook hands.

Simon grabbed a beer from the cooler and walked away from the group while they got ready for dinner. He stared off into the sunset and wished his mother was still here so he could talk to her.

Looking around to see if anyone was in listening distance, Simon cleared his throat and spoke to the red and orange sky.

"I don't want to take anything from him, Ma. Maybe I could just borrow it from his inheritance and then pay it back?" Simon felt stupid. It was all his money. But it really wasn't.

She would have wanted him to use his father's money. Simon knew that. She'd want Simon to stay in her cabin. They had gone there to get away from it all a few times. It had been good when she hadn't been drunk.

"I'll fix it up good as new," Simon told the sky.

He'd split the difference with the old man. But only because he wouldn't be able to get the cabin ready in time for Christmas without it. Besides, he liked the idea of spending time with Merry in the cabin, where they both had great memories, instead of the house of horrors where his father was in every corner.

"You'd like Merry," he said. "I wish I had brought her around when we were dating." But Simon hadn't known if his mother would have been sober. It shamed him now when he realized he had been embarrassed by her.

"I'm sorry," he said to the sky.

Maybe if he said it often enough, she'd hear him on the wind or something.

Simon finished his beer and went back to the ranch house for dinner.

THE NEXT MORNING, the retreat group was sent over to Trent Campbell's rodeo school to give the barns a good cleaning and to build extra wooden stands for the crowd they were expecting. Today, the bull riders were practicing. The bullfighters were dressed in their clown outfits and it felt more like a rodeo than a work day.

All around Simon, people had side bets going on about everything, from who was going to stay on the longest to who was going to get thrown off the bull.

Simon hoped to get a glimpse of Merry and maybe steal a kiss now that the cat was out of the Instagram bag. From what he saw looking at the reels the ranch hands showed him, no one really cared who he was. They just assumed he was a regular cowboy. It suited him. Maybe that's who he could become, now that he was no longer an inmate.

Merry hadn't shown up, but he did get to see Trent Campbell—who had retired from bull riding—get on a big, nasty beast named Precious. Simon wondered if the bull had come from the same ranch as Tinkerbell and Tweety Pie. What was even more entertaining than seeing Trent back on a bull, was watching Trent's wife scream at him the entire time that he was out of his damned mind.

Trent might be crazy, but he also went the full eight seconds before launching himself off the bull and landing on his feet.

He was a legend.

Charlie came over to him as the group was heading back to work. "Can I talk to you for a minute?"

"Sure." The retreat team was working around the ranch this afternoon, so he didn't have to worry about being late in the saddle when the other ranch hands rode back out to fix the fencing. That was on his duty chart for tomorrow. And if the blisters on Chris's hands were any indication, Simon needed to get a sturdy pair of work gloves.

He hoped the contractors hadn't changed their mind about the job or raised their estimate. The cabin was in rough shape.

"There's been a woman trying to reach you. She's been calling my office and has been making a pest of herself."

"Me?" Simon said, confused. "Who is it?"

Reaching into his pocket, Charlie pulled out a scrap of paper and handed it to him. "Joyce Davidson."

Joyce? He only knew one Joyce. Her name had been Reynolds at the time, though. The paper had her phone number on it. "Did she say what she wanted?"

"She said it was urgent that she speak to you. She didn't leave much more information than that. I'd appreciate it if you'd give her a call so she'll stop bugging my secretary and anyone else who answers the phone."

"Yeah, I'll call her. I've got a few seconds now."

Charlie nodded and moved on.

Taking a deep breath, Simon called the number. It went to voicemail, but he recognized Joyce's voice right away.

"I'm not sure what's so urgent, but give me a call at this number. Stop bugging the Lincoln Group," he said and hung up.

It had to have something to do with his father. Did she want money? The house? He'd sell it to her if that's what she was looking for, but she didn't have a leg to stand on if she thought she stood to inherit it. His dad had left her a lump sum in the will. She wasn't entitled to anything else.

He hoped he could fob her off on the attorneys because he didn't need his stepmother back in his life. Not that she had ever been a motherly figure to him.

Chapter Eleven

MERRY KNEW IT was childish to avoid her mother's and sisters' phone calls, but she truly didn't want to deal with the drama. She was a grown-ass woman who could date whomever she wanted to. Of course, that argument sounded a lot better in her head than it would have, if she'd dared to say that to her mother.

Merry was having a leisurely breakfast staring into her cup of coffee, but not finding any answers in the murky brew. It wasn't like it was a Magic 8 Ball. It was just a good cup of coffee. But a girl could hope. As she was finishing the last drop, over the rim of the mug, she saw her mother burst into the dining room of the bed-and-breakfast flanked by June and April.

Fuck.

"Let's not do this here," Merry said as they circled around her.

"You chose the venue when you didn't answer our phone calls," June said.

"I've been busy."

April flashed her phone screen at her. On an Instagram rodeo channel that they all followed, there was a picture of

Simon and Merry laughing in the food line at the drive-in movie. And then there was one of them inside the Corvette.

Whoops, the windshield hadn't been as fogged up as she thought.

"Not your best side," June said snarkily.

"I beg to differ. I bet there's a few other people who disagree with you too." Six thousand likes to be exact.

"I didn't raise you to make a scene in public," her mother said.

"Then, let's not make one now." Merry got up from the table, threw down a tip, and calmly walked out of the restaurant area. She didn't see any cell phone cameras flashing, and that was a good thing. It was still early and a weekday morning, but that didn't mean that there weren't any fans out there looking to capture some Grayson drama.

"Let's go back home and dish this out," Merry said, hauling herself into her truck.

"Don't think we won't chase you down if you try to make a run for it," April said as she, June, and her mother got into her mother's beat-up four-door sedan.

Even if Merry did want to delay the inevitable, she knew that her truck could pass anything on the highway except the gas station. Her mother's clunker would catch up to her as soon as she pulled in to refuel because it went through gas like Raphael went through oats.

After parking outside of her mother's trailer, she walked over to the small corral that was attached to it. She put her hand through the slats and rubbed the nose of her mother's pony, Tulip.

"I bet you miss Raphael and Athena," Merry said. Part of her balked at the expense of boarding the horses at the Three Sisters Ranch, but it made sense and was more relaxing for the horses. Rather than trailering the horses to and from there until the charity rodeo, they got to stay in one place. After the rodeo, she and June would bring their horses home. But for now, Tulip was the only horse in the corral.

"Simon fucking Reynolds?" her mother screeched, slamming the car door and stalking over to Merry.

"Simon Reynolds," June said, shaking her head with a big smile on her face.

"Simon Reynolds?" April said, her hands on her hips.

With a sigh, Merry turned around and leaned her back against the fence.

April winced. "Don't turn your back on her."

"Tulip knows better than to start anything with me," Merry said. "Raphael would stomp her into the ground."

"Raphael isn't here," April said, crossing her arms over her chest. "It would serve you right if she bit you on the arm."

"Tulip doesn't bite," their mother said.

They all rolled their eyes. Tulip would bite if she thought she could get away with it. But Merry and June had been sneaking her carrots and sugar cubes forever. April had been too afraid to feed Tulip, so Merry and June were Tulip's favorites. Tulip nuzzled Merry's elbow. Placing her hand in her pocket, Merry pulled out a sugar cube that she had taken from the breakfast table.

"Yes, Simon and I have hooked up again." Merry wiped

her hand off on her jeans after Tulip slobbered all over it. "Not that you needed me to confirm that. You probably recognized the car and him from the photos online."

"He's with Charlie's retreat, isn't he?" June asked. "Esteban mentioned a guy named Simon who was doing really well. But I haven't had a chance to go over and check out the convicts."

"Ex-convicts," Merry said. "Simon and the rest of them are out on parole."

"Out on parole again," her mother said. "How many times has that boy been in jail?"

"Too many times."

"You got that right. What are you thinking dating a man like him?" her mother said.

Merry could bring up that her mother hadn't always made the best choices in choosing the men in her life, either, but she had a feeling that would only escalate the situation.

"It's complicated. He's had a rough life."

"So have we all, but we didn't resort to stealing cars or breaking and entering."

"About that," Merry said. "The car and the house were his father's. His father was the one who shot at us and had him arrested."

"He shot at his own son?" Her mother looked confused. "He pressed charges against him?"

"Yeah. It was a control thing," Merry said, not wanting to give away all of Simon's secrets but she didn't see another way around it. "Simon was acting out. He was upset about his parents' divorce and was trying to hurt his father. His father thought he would teach Simon a lesson, and it back-fired."

"Are you saying he called the police on his own son?" April asked.

"Not only did he call the cops on his own son, he got the judge to send his son to jail. But things went to shit after that. Then when he got out, he was so full of anger that he did some stupid things and got sent right back in."

"Didn't his father try to help him?" June asked.

"I don't know," Merry said. "He never spoke to him again. His father died a few months ago, while Simon was still in prison. He left him the house and the car."

"So, he's rich?" her mother said. "That seems a little too good to be true. Are you sure you're not being scammed?"

"Well, I haven't seen the will. But he's driving the Corvette, and nobody tried to shoot at us when we were in the house."

"If you have the house, why were you screwing around at the drive-in?" April asked.

June, Merry, and their mother looked at April and shook their heads.

"Cole needs to step up his game," Merry said.

April gasped. "No, he does not. Just because the three of you are exhibitionists, that doesn't mean I am."

"It's not exhibition, it's spontaneity," June said.

"You call it spontaneity, the rest of us call it having to enter the barn with our hands over our eyes," April said.

Merry was glad that the focus was momentarily taken off of her. She looked at her mother, and Penny seemed less likely to blow her top now. Merry could tell she was thinking about what she had just heard.

"How could a man do that to his own son?" Penny asked.

"How could a man walk away and leave his daughters?" Merry countered, unable to stop herself.

Penny winced. "I haven't chosen the best men in my life, I'll admit. That's why I'm so concerned about Simon. Cole and Esteban are good men. I'd hoped you'd find someone like them to be with."

"Simon is a good guy too, once you get to know him."

"But how well do you know him?" April said. "The last time you saw him, you were both in high school."

"I'm not saying that we're going to run away to Tahiti and get married," Merry said. "We're just dating and seeing where it goes."

"It looks pretty serious to me," April said.

"That's because you're a prude," Merry said.

"I am not a prude," April said. "I just like having sex in a bed, instead of a car."

"Don't knock it until you've tried it," Merry retorted.

"I don't like it." Her mother sighed. "But I don't have to. I just don't want to see you hurt, or worse, get caught up in another crazy scene where some asshole is shooting at you."

"Well, since the asshole who shot at me the last time is dead, I don't think that's going to be a problem."

"What is Simon planning to do now that he's out of prison?" April asked.

"He's still figuring that out," Merry said.

"You can't count on this being permanent," her mother said. "Not when he's figuring his own life out."

"I never count on anything being permanent," Merry said. "There hasn't been a man in my life who hasn't abandoned me."

Penny winced again, and Merry felt bad. That hadn't been a shot at her mother. It was just the honest truth.

"Give him a chance. I think he'll win you over," Merry said.

"What do you really know about him?" June said. "I just don't want you to get hurt, thinking he's the same boy you remember."

"None of us are the same people we were ten years ago."

"Yeah, but he spent the last ten years in prison. You spent it on the rodeo circuit. Now that he's free, he's going to want to sow some wild oats," Penny said. "I don't want you to get your heart involved, and then have him break it when he moves on."

"Even if he does move on," Merry said. "There are ways we can still keep in touch. Technology is our friend."

Penny frowned. "You deserve so much more."

"I appreciate that," Merry said, trying to hold on to her temper. The same could be said about her mother and all of her boyfriends. But Merry was trying not to be confrontational. "Simon invited all of us to his mother's cabin for Christmas Day to celebrate with him."

"What's his mother have to say about that?" Penny asked.

"She passed away. He's fixing the cabin up and wanted the Grayson family to be his first guests."

Penny was already shaking her head. "No. I don't think that's a good idea."

"I want to spend Christmas with him. I would really like it if you and everyone would just move the Christmas celebration from wherever we were going to have it, to Simon's place."

"There's a lot of us," April said. "Does Simon know what he's getting himself into?"

"I have all my plans," Penny said. "I'm making my own lasagna in my own kitchen, and then if the weather is nice, I'm going set up the tables outside and have a big buffet spread."

"You can do all of that at Simon's house, except we'd be inside, and we wouldn't have to worry about the weather. The cabin will fit all of us." Barely. It would be a cozy Christmas, that was for dang sure.

"I'm game," June said. Bless her.

Penny shook her head. "No. It's too much of an imposition. We're all strangers. It wouldn't feel comfortable in a strange place."

Merry managed to hold on to her temper, but just barely. "All right then. How about I bring Simon to our Christmas celebration?"

Penny was already shaking her head before she finished her sentence. "We're going to be pushing max capacity as it is with your sisters' boyfriends."

"Just a minute ago, you said it would be outside."

"But that's only if the weather is nice," Penny said hastily.

"You know what I think, Mama? I think you just don't want to spend Christmas with Simon."

"All right, you're right. I don't. He was a thief who almost got you shot and after ten years of no contact, he's suddenly fogging up drive-in windows with you. I don't like him. I don't trust him. Christmas is a special time for family. And while I'm sorry that his daddy did him wrong, it sounds like he was a wild child who deserved a hard lesson."

"A hard lesson is getting a switch to the backside or being grounded and being unable to go to the prom. Being sent to jail when you're an eighteen-year-old kid who was tried as a man is a bit more than a hard lesson. His daddy fucked up. Simon lost his mom while he was in prison. He's all on his own." Merry put her hands on her hips and finally let her temper out. "I came back here to spend Christmas and my birthday with my family. Can't you meet me halfway here?"

"Well, I can see there's no talking to you." Penny turned on her heel and went inside.

"Now you've done it," April said.

"Done what? Your boyfriends were all welcomed into the family with open arms. All I'm asking for is for you guys to come to dinner at my boyfriend's place."

"Merry, you've known him for three days," April said.

"I've known him since he was eighteen. So have all of you."

"Even back then, he wasn't the type to knock on the door and make small talk with us while you got ready," April said. "From what I remember, he laid on the horn with heavy metal music blasting. And then you would run out the door and didn't come back until well past curfew."

"I was just a kid," Merry said defensively.

"You were both kids," June said, mildly. "I think we should give Simon another chance."

"Good luck convincing Mama with that," April said.

"I don't have to convince her. I'm spending Christmas with Simon at his place. You guys are welcome to join us. But if you don't want to, I understand."

"Mama is going to be very hurt if you don't show up for Christmas," April said.

"I would be very hurt if you all don't show up at Simon's," Merry countered.

"Don't put us in the middle," June said. "We're on your side. We just don't want Christmas to be a battlefield."

"It won't be a battlefield if you just come to Simon's house. I'm going to go all out decorating. And I do want all of us to be together in a nice place. Not cramped together in an old tin can." She waved her hand at her mother's double-wide.

"Don't call our home a tin can," April said.

"All I'm saying is trying to fit eight people in there is going to be tight."

"I'll work on Mama," April said. "Maybe, when she's had time to cool down and think about it, she'll reconsider."

"What planet are you living on?" June said. "She's not going to change her mind. Thanks for ruining Christmas, Merry." June stomped back to her truck and drove away in a dust cloud of kicked-up gravel.

"How am I the bad guy?" Merry asked.

April placed a hand on her arm. "There aren't any good guys or bad guys. You and Mama are just too stubborn."

"I don't see why we can't compromise."

"If it had been anyone other than Simon Reynolds," April said, "she would've been overjoyed. But because it's Simon, you're going to have an uphill battle. It's just one day, Merry. Not even a full day, if you don't want it to be. Just come for lunch. Stay a few hours and then go to Simon's for dinner."

"I've got to go," Merry said, giving April a quick hug.

She'd figure something out. If her mother could accept Luke back, time and time again, for Merry's birthday and Christmas, she'd eventually come around to accepting Simon. But for now, Merry had to put all of that out of her mind and get some more practice time in. Once that was done, she could concentrate on the holidays. Maybe she'd get some inspiration at the Christmas parade and tree lighting. Those had always been great times that had led into an epic birthday and holiday.

Chapter Twelve

S IMON FOUND HIMSELF in the uncomfortable position of standing in a crowd on Main Street, waiting for the Christmas parade to start. Charlie had gone out of his way to arrange that all of the retreat members got the morning off to be here. It was hokey, but they got to sleep in later than usual and the few hours off work made him feel as if he was playing hooky from school again.

He saw a few of the guys snacking on candy apples and hot fresh pretzels. Simon had passed on them, but he couldn't resist the cheesecake on the stick from Char-Pie Bakery. If he got a stomachache later while he was out riding, it would've been well worth it.

Simon hated being crowded together with all the other people. The only good thing was that Merry was holding his hand and standing close enough that he could smell her floral shampoo.

He nuzzled her ear and claimed a quick kiss. "I'll be right back. I've got to meet Charlie at the bank so I can give him money for the contractors to fix up the cabin."

"Remember," she said. "I can help too."

"I'm going to take you up on that, don't worry."

Reluctantly, he left her and threaded his way through the crowds. He hated how close everyone was to him and didn't relax until he had stepped into the bank. Simon felt shaky and he was sweating. Pulling a handkerchief out of his pocket, he wiped his forehead.

Charlie was waiting in the lobby for him.

"Hey," he said, walking over to him. But before he reached Charlie, Penny Grayson stepped in front of him.

"What are you doing here?" she asked, crossing her arms. "You're not planning on robbing the place, are you?"

Penny wasn't a quiet woman and people looked up at them. Tension filled the room. Out of the corner of his eye, he saw one of the guards casually drop his hand to the butt of his pistol.

Simon resisted the urge to lash out at her with angry words. Tightening his jaw, he kept a lid on his temper. "No, ma'am," he forced out. "I'm here to do some banking, same as you."

"I don't trust you," she said, eyes narrowed.

"You don't have to," he said as evenly as he could and tried to step around her.

"You're going to hurt my daughter," Penny said, walking with him.

"That is not my intention. I care deeply for Merry." Simon wished he had said those words to Merry first, but her mother had set him off his game.

"She doesn't need you," Penny said.

"I am aware of that." Simon looked over her head at Charlie and gave him a glance that he hoped could be interpreted as "A little help here?"

"What are your intentions toward my daughter?"

Simon didn't really need this crap. But there were two people ahead of him in line and Penny didn't seem to be in a hurry to move along.

"Your daughter and I are dating."

"Are you going to be staying in Last Stand?"

"I don't know."

"Do you have a job lined up?"

"Not yet."

"So you're just having a good time and then you're going to leave her high and dry?"

Simon had a feeling that Penny's own experiences were coloring her opinion on this, but he wasn't about to point that out to her.

"Your daughter and I are seeing each other. It's none of your business what goes on between us." He tried to be polite, but it was difficult.

"You are going to hurt her—I just know it. And I don't want to see her fall to pieces again when you leave."

Guilt slashed through him. "Merry and I are no longer kids. The situation now is different from the situation then."

"Is it?" Penny blew out a big sigh. "I don't want you to get Merry in trouble if you backslide into your old ways."

Okay, that was enough. He whirled on her, about to explode when Charlie's hand thumped heavy on his shoulder and turned him back around so he was facing the person in front of him in line.

"Now, Penny," Charlie said. "Don't you think you're

being a little bit hard on the boy?"

"His father shot at my daughter."

Simon felt Charlie tense. It probably brought back bad memories of when Charlie's family had been shot at, but Charlie rallied quickly. "That was a long time ago, and Braxton Reynolds is no longer around for a repeat performance."

"He stole a car," Penny hissed.

Fuck it. He whirled around again. "I stole a lot of them," Simon snapped before he could stop himself.

Charlie closed his eyes and winced.

There were more audible gasps, but Simon didn't care.

"I went to prison, and I did my time. I'm rehabilitated, and I'm trying to get my life back in order. I was a dumb kid with too much pride. If I could change my past, I would. But I can't, so I'm just doing the best I can. I'd appreciate it if you'd back off."

"I'll back off all right, as soon as you back off my daughter."

Simon reached into his pocket.

"I have a pistol," Penny said, backpedaling and reaching into her purse.

The security guards shifted position and concentrated on Penny.

Simon pulled out his phone and dialed Merry. "Hey, you need to come into the bank. Your mother is making a scene."

"What are you doing?" Penny said, looking between him and the security guards.

"I'm getting your daughter to talk some sense into you

before you do something that you're going to regret," Simon said.

"Penny," Charlie soothed. "Take your hand out of your purse slowly, and let's go get a cup of coffee or something."

"I'm not the criminal here. He is," Penny said.

"Right now, you're the one in danger of being arrested." Charlie held out his hand and Penny reluctantly took it. He led her over to the seating area in the lobby and sat down next to her, talking quietly.

After a few more tense moments, everything went back to normal in the bank and Simon was relieved to move one more person closer in line for the teller. Then Merry stormed in.

"What the hell is going on here?" she asked.

And now they were the center of attention again. Simon looked up at the ceiling, wishing he had never gone to the bank this morning at all.

"Calm down," Penny said.

"This is calm," Merry said, seething.

Charlie stood up. "Ladies, why don't we take this outside?"

"In a moment," Merry said and walked up to Simon. "What did she say to you?"

Shaking his head, he said, "It doesn't matter."

"I'm sorry."

"Don't you apologize for me," Penny said.

"Mama, butt out."

Charlie succeeded in walking a few steps with Penny toward the door, but she stopped in her tracks, waiting for

Merry.

Merry turned back to him. "We'll talk in a bit once you've finished your business." She cupped his face and gave him a satisfying kiss.

"She's just concerned about you," he said, holding her close. "But she was being a righteous bitch."

"I heard that," Penny snarled.

"You were being a righteous bitch," Charlie said.

Penny snatched her hand away from the crook of Charlie's arm and strode out the front door.

"I'll handle this," Merry said when Charlie went to follow.

The whole situation made him sick to his stomach. He tried to see it from Penny's point of view. If the situation had been reversed, his mother wouldn't have been too thrilled with Merry either. Nothing that Penny had said to him had been invalid, but it sucked to have his business aired in a public place. And small towns being what they were, he was sure he hadn't heard the last of this.

Finally, it was his turn and Charlie leaned up against the counter as Simon handed the teller the two withdrawal slips he had filled out.

The teller called up the account his mother had set up for him. "How do you want the cash?"

Simon looked at Charlie.

"Hundreds are fine."

She counted out twenty-five one-hundred-dollar bills and put them into an envelope. Simon had a moment's twinge of giving it to Charlie who had admitted to being a con man. But Charlie had played it square with him so far, and it was about time that Simon started trusting people again. With a sigh, he handed it to Charlie who counted it before slipping it into his pocket.

Then the teller called up the account that his father's lawyer had set up for him. She frowned at the screen. "I'm sorry, sir. I have to get the manager. Can you have a seat in that office over there?" She pointed to one of the offices in the corner.

"Why? What's going on?" Simon asked, the sick feeling in his stomach coming back. Had his father found a way to screw with him from beyond the grave?

"I'm not sure, but the account is flagged so I can't access it. Only a manager can. It should only be a moment. I apologize for the inconvenience."

Simon's gaze darted around the bank, but no one seemed to be paying any attention to him. The guards had gone back to their posts and had slightly bored expressions on their faces. He and Charlie went into the office and sat down.

"Do you think this has anything to do with what Penny Grayson said?" Simon asked.

"I doubt it," Charlie said. "More likely is there's a snafu with the account transfer."

"Figures," Simon muttered. It served him right for trying to access his father's money. "Don't worry. I've got enough in my other account for the repairs."

"I'm not worried," Charlie said.

A few moments later, a man who Simon didn't recognize came in. He was wearing a sharp suit and held out his hand to Simon. Rising from the chair, Simon shook it.

"Please, Mr. Reynolds, sit. I'm sorry to have kept you waiting. Your father was a valued customer of ours and we're looking forward to a long relationship with you as well."

"So what's the problem?" Simon asked, still feeling a little raw from the encounter.

The manager handed Simon a padded envelope. "Your father wanted you to have this when you accessed the account for the first time."

That canny old bastard. Simon turned the envelope over and over. It felt like a lot of pages. "What is it?"

"He didn't say, but he was adamant that you have it. Perhaps it's important paperwork or passcodes or something."

"Right," Simon said. "Thanks."

"And here is your withdrawal." The manager handed him an envelope.

Simon wordlessly passed it to Charlie. Yeah, this was going to be a loan. He was going to pay back the twenty-five hundred dollars to this account as soon as he got a job and was settled. He was only taking the money because he wanted to fix up the cabin sooner rather than later.

"I appreciate it." Simon tapped the envelope.

"Enjoy the parade," the manager said.

Charlie didn't say anything until they were out of the bank. "Are you okay? I can drive you back to the ranch if you'd rather skip the festivities."

He wanted to get into his car and drive fast and far away. Or even get on a horse and ride out into the great wide open.

But he needed to see Merry.

"Nah, I'm good. Are your guys all set to start work at the cabin?"

"They'll be there this afternoon."

"Thanks," Simon said, looking at the ground and then up at him. "For everything."

Charlie squeezed his shoulder. "It's not going to be easy, but you handled that well. Penny will come around. She's not a mean woman. She's just very overprotective of her daughters."

"She has reason to be in my case," Simon said. He had been a fool to think differently.

"I don't think so, and more importantly, Merry doesn't either."

"Yeah," he said. "See you later."

Pushing through the crowd, feeling like ants were crawling all over him, he found Merry standing by a vendor selling hot chocolate with peppermint stick stirrers. When she saw him approaching, she bought two of them and handed him one.

He took his and was surprised to find the deep rich flavor wasn't too sweet.

She pulled out a flask from her jacket pocket and added two splashes of whiskey to both of their hot chocolates. He probably should have stopped her, but it felt a bit like old times and he could use a drink. Besides, by the time he got back to the Three Sisters Ranch, he'd be completely sober.

"I am so sorry she ambushed you like that," Merry said. "She was out of line, and I told her so."

"She caught me off guard," Simon said. "I could have handled it better."

"You handled it just fine. I'm mortified that she confronted you like that."

"Don't be. You warned me that she hated me."

"She's being irrational, and I told her that, too."

"I bet that went over well."

"She knows she overreacted, and she's embarrassed by it. But it will be a while before she settles down and apologizes."

"I don't need her to apologize."

"I do," Merry said. "And I totally understand if you want to cancel Christmas."

"Cancel Christmas?" He couldn't help smiling. "I don't think I have that kind of pull with Santa."

She leaned her head against his shoulder. "You know what I mean."

He put his arm around her. "My offer still stands. Even if it turns out to be just you and me, it will be the best Christmas I've had in over ten years."

"I always loved this time of the year," she said. "I was supposed to be in Tahiti until New Year's."

"What happened?" he asked.

"Broncs happened," Merry said. "I got hurt and my friends left for the island without me."

"Some friends," he said.

"I was really bummed about settling for Last Stand instead of Tahiti, but then I found out you were here." She squeezed him. "I don't care what my mother says. You make me happy."

He swallowed the lump in his throat. "You make me happy too."

"Do you remember watching the parade when we were kids?"

"I remember wishing we were alone instead." In fact, he wondered if he could convince her to head on back to the retreat center with him for a little private time.

But the parade was starting. They'd have a hard time leaving now.

The town had gone all out decorating the floats. The members of the marching band played Christmas carols, and they were all dressed like elves.

"It's all rather wholesome, don't you think?" He sipped the spiked chocolate. It was damned good. And it went a long way in numbing the ugly scene at the bank. Simon wished he could assure Penny that he'd rather cut off his leg than to hurt Merry again. But she had brought up two very good points. He didn't know what he was going to do after the retreat—he could be leaving Last Stand to find a job. And he didn't have the right to expect anything from Merry.

"You could use a little wholesome in your life," she said. "We both could."

She wasn't wrong. Still, he didn't like being in the crowd, even though standing with the people of Last Stand was a far cry away from being in a prison yard. He wished he could relax, but with everyone crushed in so close, that was impossible. He forced himself to concentrate on the gaily decorated procession. The Peach Queen, in her enormous ball gown, waved to the crowd and tossed out peach candies.

He managed to catch one, but Merry got smacked in the forehead with a few.

"Ow, I think she was aiming at me," Merry said.

"Did you ever want to be the Peach Queen?" Simon asked.

"When I was five," Merry retorted. "After that, the only queen I wanted to be was queen of the rodeo."

"I remember." Merry had always been horse crazy. She hadn't had Raphael at that time, but all she talked about had been saving enough money to buy her own barrel-racing horse.

She had done so well in junior rodeos and in high school classes that she had gotten a rodeo scholarship. And then she was on her way. Maybe if he hadn't gone to prison, he still would've lost her.

He likely would have stayed here in Last Stand, or maybe in Whiskey River, working on a ranch. It would've been a good life, certainly one that was a lot better than his last ten years had been. But he wouldn't have seen Merry a lot because of all the traveling she had done pursuing her dream. Would they have survived? Would he have come to resent her?

Oh, who was he kidding? His father would have never allowed his son to be a manual laborer. Although *allowed* had always been a contentious point between the two of them. Simon had to wonder if he would have eventually caved in to the pressure and accepted an office job where he was paid a lot for doing a little because he was the boss's son.

At eighteen, maybe that would have appealed to him, but

now that he was closer to thirty, he knew that he didn't want to rely on his father or his handouts. It would be easy to keep his father's house and live off his father's money for a while. It was a better idea, though, to sell it and give the money away so he could put Braxton Reynolds behind him. After all, he'd given away his dad's money to charity before. And then Simon would be free to put down roots somewhere else, where there was no memory of his father.

But where? And what would he do when he got there?

He touched the envelope he had stuffed in his jacket pocket. What the hell was in it? Was it a copy of the package the lawyer had given him that he had destroyed? Could it be print-outs of all the letters he wrote to Simon while he was in prison? Was it stock certificates or cash money?

Simon didn't want to open it. But maybe he wouldn't destroy this one. Not yet, anyway.

He watched Merry enjoy the parade. It was nice to see it through her eyes—her wonder, her joy of the season. Something in his heart shifted. He could watch her for hours and the crowd no longer mattered.

After the parade, Simon was still feeling warm and mellow from the whiskey in the hot chocolate. He knew he had to start heading back to the Three Sisters Ranch, but he was reluctant to do so. It wasn't that he didn't like his job. He did. It beat the heck out of being in prison and working in the cafeteria. But he was just starting to relax in the crowd of people, and he wanted to explore that feeling a little bit more. Out on the ranch, he worked either all alone or with a partner. He preferred it that way, and he knew that he worked best when no one else was watching him.

But that wouldn't let him integrate into society. Standing here, doing "normal things," was what would help him get acclimated. That, and being with Merry made it seem like he could succeed in the outside world.

Main Street would be blocked off for the weekend while Christmas booths popped up, selling everything from ornaments to handmade goods. None of that appealed to him. But he got a kick out of watching Merry's face light up when she saw a cowboy gnome, with a huge ten-gallon hat covering most of his face and resting on his large round nose.

"He kind of looks a little like you," Simon said, deadpan.

"I knew I should've gotten my nose done when I had the chance," she said.

He kissed her nose. "I like your nose. Don't you dare change it."

"Yeah, I suppose if I was going to get my nose broken, it would be in a bar fight and not by a plastic surgeon," Merry said.

"I'd try to avoid bar fights too."

"Smart idea."

They continued walking among the stalls and Merry asked, "Are there any Christmas decorations in your mom's cabin?"

"I don't think so, but if there were, they've likely been ruined. The attic and the basement had severe water damage."

"That's rough," Merry said. "How about in your dad's house?"

"I wouldn't know. The decorations appeared December first and disappeared December twenty-six. For all I know, Joyce rented the décor for the holiday."

"Maybe after the tree lighting tonight, we can go back and see what's in the attic."

"I can think of some better things we can do with that time. It's got to be an early night though. I have to be back at the retreat center at a decent hour so I can get up and cook breakfast with Luis tomorrow."

"What's on the menu?"

"Scrambled eggs and cheese, bacon, sausage, biscuits."

"How domestic of you," Merry said. "Can I come?"

"I'm sure the boys won't mind. Is four thirty a.m. good for you?"

"As my bedtime?"

"No. Showered, dressed, and seated at the table."

Merry shuddered. "I could never be a ranch hand. How do you stand it?"

"It's just a matter of getting used to the routines. The prison had us up at daybreak and into our respective jobs around dawn."

Merry put the gnome down and moved on to look at tree skirts. "How did you celebrate the holidays in there?" she asked, keeping her voice low.

She didn't have to bother. By tonight, everyone in Last Stand would have heard about the scene in the bank, and know that Merry was dating an ex-con. But the shopkeeper was chatting with her neighbor and not paying them any attention.

"Sometimes, we had better food. But not always. We got time off from work if we attended a religious service. I wasn't much of a believer, but I found that it helped a bit, even if it was just for a quick snooze or meditation."

"What about before prison? What do you remember about Christmas when you were a kid? We never really talked about this. I should have invited you to celebrate my birthday at the very least."

"I wasn't much of a family person back then."

He still wasn't. Simon got that itchy feeling between his shoulder blades again, and he looked around but nobody seemed to be paying any attention to them. They moved on to another stall where there were all different-sized Christmas ornament balls used to make bracelets and earrings. Merry put one on and twisted her wrist to make the bracelet jingle. Simon didn't want to think about his childhood, but he supposed this was also part of him becoming acclimated into polite society—talking and shit.

"When I was a kid, long before I met you, my dad traveled during the holidays, so it was mostly just me and my mom."

"Did you have any traditions? Like did you open up presents on Christmas Eve or Christmas morning?"

"Christmas Eve," he said. "Because Christmas morning, my mom was in the kitchen cooking. We ate leftovers until New Year's. On the rare occasions my father was home, Christmas Day was about impressing his business clients who were traveling and couldn't be with their own family for Christmas. I always had to be on my best behavior." Simon made a face. "No kid should have to wear a suit on Christmas."

Merry nodded. "It's an all-day pajama fest at the Graysons. We open our presents Christmas morning because Christmas Eve is all about me and my birthday. Did you have a big house like the one he moved into after the divorce?"

"No, but it was big enough, I suppose. We never had more than two or three guests for Christmas."

"Did you have a real tree or an artificial one?"

"What is this, twenty questions, Christmas edition?" he asked, grinning at her to take the sting out of his words.

"It's important I know these things for our party."

Our party. Who would have thought that he'd be hosting a Christmas party a few weeks after getting out of prison? And inviting someone who truly disliked him. Maybe, he could be a little selfish and wish that Penny and her attitude would stay home.

"A real tree," he said.

Merry took a deep breath, as if she was smelling it. "I've always wanted a real tree."

"My mom hated it. It shed pine needles all over the place, and she was always worried that it was a fire hazard because of all the candles that my father insisted were lit overnight."

"Were the candles bayberry scented or vanilla?"

"I don't remember." He stared at her bemusement. When she asked questions like that, she seemed like such a girly girl, which was a totally different side of her than Simon had seen before. He was enchanted.

"I bet if you smelled it, you'd remember it."

"I guess?" he said, surprised when she grabbed him by the hand and dragged him to a candle stand. They spent the next ten minutes with her uncapping and thrusting candles under his nose. The smells weren't bad, but all of them, in such a short amount of time, were giving him a headache.

When he turned to sneeze, he saw Charlie approaching them.

"We've got to get going," Charlie said.

Simon felt a mixture of disappointment and relief. He wanted to stick around and enjoy this crazy Christmas side of Merry, but on the other hand, he was eager to get back to work and get away from the crowded streets.

"I'll see you tonight," he said, leaning down to kiss her cheek.

She grabbed his face and kissed him smack dab on the lips. It was a steamy kiss that lasted so long, Charlie had to clear his throat to get their attention.

"See you tonight for the tree lighting, cowboy," she said with a saucy wink at Charlie.

Chapter Thirteen

SIMON WAS BONE-TIRED after a long day in the saddle and the emotional start of the day at the bank. But he gamely stood next to Merry, shoulder to shoulder, stifling a yawn. The mayor gave a speech. Santa Claus came out and greeted the crowd. He looked suspiciously like Police Chief Highwater in a fake beard and a padded red velvet suit. Simon fought to keep his eyes open. He should probably get a cup of coffee, otherwise he was going to waste his time with Merry tonight sleeping. His body still remembered the arousing kisses from this morning, and he wanted to explore that a bit more. But he was fading fast.

"Do you want to go inside the library and check out the giving tree?" Merry asked.

"What's the giving tree?" He vaguely remembered a book where a tree gave up everything for a little boy. It always made him feel uncomfortable because his own father could have written a book called *The Taking Tree*.

"Instead of ornaments, the Daughters of Last Stand hang tags with Christmas present requests from kids, mostly teens, who wouldn't be getting presents this year. You pick a tag off the tree and get the requested gift that's on the tag. Then you wrap it and put it back under the tree with the tag on it. The DOLS will make sure it gets to the right person. It's a great idea, because everybody wants to give toys to the little kids. But after a certain age, the older kids just get socks and underwear."

Simon had already bought a toy for the toy drive, but this sounded like a good idea too. "Sure," Simon said. "Let's check it out."

It reminded him of his Robin Hood days where he would steal from his father and give to the charities that would've made his father's head explode had he known where the money had been going. Of course, there came a time when you had to stop letting your parents control all your decisions. Simon was still trying to work himself toward finding his own way, but so far, he hadn't been successful.

Watching Merry look at every tag made him realize that she had been one of the kids whose wishes had been on the tree.

"Let's take all of them," he said.

Merry had been looking at five in her hand, trying to decide which ones she wanted to choose.

"All five?" she asked.

"No," Simon said, starting to remove all of the tags hanging on the giving tree. "I mean all of them."

Merry gaped at him. "We really should leave some for other people to take. People love doing this. It makes them feel good."

"Then I guess the teens are just going to have to come up with another present that they want."

She almost tackled him to the ground with the force of her hug. He held her tightly as her body shivered and she hiccupped.

"I'm not crying," she said. "I must be allergic to the incense that they're burning in the fire outside."

Nobody was burning incense, but he didn't correct her.

"You're going to have to go shopping with me on my day off this week. I'm going to need help getting all of this stuff," he said.

"You got it. You know what?" she said excitedly. "We should get my sisters and my mother involved, too. No one can shop and find deals like my mother."

"Are you sure we can't handle it ourselves?" he asked, not eager to spend more time with Penny. But he supposed it was better to get the awkwardness out of the way now, instead of during Christmas dinner, if Penny was planning on showing up. He knew that Merry had some high expectations about this Christmas. Simon didn't want to risk having her be disappointed by any negativity that her mother had every right to feel toward him.

※

AT LEAST SIMON got to watch her ass as she climbed up the stairs to the attic. He was pretty sure that the old man had hired interior designers to come in and decorate this house for Christmas, mostly because he never remembered Joyce doing any sort of Christmas crap like that.

The attic was hot and dusty. He went over to the window and tried to lift it up. Years of neglect had sealed it shut, but he managed to muscle it open about an inch and a half. The fresh, cool night air felt good on his face. He hadn't thought that after spending all of that time in a six-by-six cell, he could get claustrophobic, but he didn't like it up here. It felt like being back in prison. He stayed by the window and took deep breaths. The naked bulb in the center of the room swung in small circles, casting everything in dim shadows.

"We should come back up during the day," he said.

"You think it's hot now?" Merry asked. "We'd have to bring up fans to keep from dying. And I don't think there's anywhere to plug them in up here."

"Just let me know if you're having trouble breathing with all of the dust being kicked up. There might even be mice nesting here." He glanced over at her to see if that would send her shrieking downstairs, but he should have known better. She wasn't even fazed.

"Probably not mice," Merry said. "A rattlesnake or two maybe."

"Rattlesnakes?" Simon heard his voice go up a few octaves, and cleared his throat.

"Yeah, depending on how sealed the place was, a snake might have come in looking for water or a place to hunt rodents and bugs. Let me know if you hear the shake of a rattlesnake tail."

"Are you putting me on?" He stared at her suspiciously.

"It happened to a friend of a friend of mine," Merry said.

He should have known that a mouse or two in the attic

wouldn't have spooked Merry. With a wary eye out for snakes, even though he thought the story was bullshit, Simon started going through the boxes. Merry pulled over an antique chair that he dimly remembered being in his mother's sewing room. She sat down and began rummaging through what was there.

"Why don't people label things?" Merry asked.

"Probably because they know what's in the box."

"How could anybody remember? There has to be at least fifty boxes up here."

She opened one plastic container and held up a dress. "Do you recognize this?"

"Dad didn't have the legs to wear a dress like that, but it doesn't look like it was something my mother or Joyce would have worn, either. Maybe he had a lady friend in between Joyce and the time he died."

"Do you think we should look for the owner of these clothes?"

"No. But we should probably go through the pockets for loose change and then just donate them. I'd have to get rid of them anyway when I sell the house."

"Seems like such a shame to sell it," she mused.

"It should go to someone who would appreciate the house and not have any baggage attached to it. I'll buy another house with the proceeds as soon as I'm settled."

"Were you thinking of going anywhere specific?" she asked casually. "Or were you planning on staying in Texas?"

"It doesn't matter to me. I'll go anywhere there's work. Although I always wanted to check out Tahiti," he said.

"Me too," she sighed.

"Do you think they have cowboys in Tahiti?"

"Can't say that I ever researched that," she said. "But I do know there are cowboys in Hawaii, on the coffee plantations. And I think they have herds of bison there as well."

"I don't think bison are a native species to Hawaii," he said.

Merry shrugged. "They've got these things called boats to deliver stuff to places like that. It's not rocket science. I imagine cargo planes filled with bison could even fly out to the islands."

"Smart-ass," he said. "Have you ever been to a rodeo in Hawaii?"

"No, but if I ever got invited to one, I'd ride as many broncs as it took to get there, and I might not go home afterward."

He smiled. "I might even get on a bull, myself, if there was a chance for me to go to Hawaii with the rodeo. Tahiti sounds nice, though. So remote and far away from everyday life."

She grinned. "It does, doesn't it? I've never been. How about you?"

"The farthest I've ever been was New York City one time during Christmas."

"That's a long way to go for a holiday trip."

"My father had business there."

"Of course," Merry said.

"We got to see the Rockettes and a Broadway show."

"Manhattan is a fun town." Merry slid the plastic container aside and picked up another tub to put on top of it. "I was there for a rodeo trade show once."

"I remember ice-skating at Rockefeller Center. Or ice falling, I should say. My father thought it was a waste of time, but my mother and I had fun." That was before she'd started drinking, and when his father had been more discreet with his mistresses. "We bought chestnuts from a street vendor. I remember they were too hot to peel at first, but once they cooled down, I made a pig of myself."

"That sounds like a nice Christmas memory." Merry rifled through the pockets of all the clothes she found, but came up empty.

"There were one or two." Simon opened up a couple more boxes and peered inside them. "All this stuff should be shredded. Although, I don't think Braxton has to worry about identity theft anymore. I suppose we could recycle the paper or just burn it all in a bonfire."

"Jackpot," Merry said, dragging a large crate into the center of the room right under the light bulb. There were several items wrapped up in newspaper, and as Merry pulled one of them out, Simon recognized the nativity scene that his mother had made in a ceramics class she had taken.

"That was my mother's," he said. "I don't know why my father has it. He wasn't very religious. And he certainly didn't harbor any sentimental feelings toward it. Why didn't he just chuck it?"

"It's beautiful," she said. "It's hand-painted and signed by the artist." She pointed out his mother's signature. "Maybe, he thought it would be worth something, someday?"

"Doubtful. My mother made that."

Merry clasped a ceramic cow to her chest. "Perfect," she sighed. "This will go under the tree. Or did you guys put it somewhere else?"

Simon had to think back to the last Christmas he remembered seeing the set. He couldn't have been more than ten or twelve. "Yeah, we put it under the tree. That would be a nice new memory to have."

"Okay bring this down into the living room and keep it separate from the totes that you're giving away."

"Yes, ma'am." Simon carried a few boxes down to the living room.

When he got back up into the attic, Merry asked, "Have you heard back from the contractors who are working on your mom's cabin?"

"Not yet, but I expect Charlie will give me the rundown tomorrow or the next day."

"Do you think it'll be ready in time for Christmas?"

Simon chuckled. "I think that might take a Christmas miracle."

"It's the time of year for them," she said. "Is there another miracle you'd like to manifest?"

"I want to start the new year a free man." He found another box of Christmas ornaments and sat down on the dusty floor to look at them.

"But you are free. Are you afraid that your parole is going to be revoked?"

"No. That's not going to happen. I already have the baddest car around. I don't need to steal another one."

Merry rolled her eyes.

"And I don't need to steal my father's money anymore, to spend it in ways that would give him a heart attack, if he was still alive."

"Like the giving tree?"

"Exactly. He wasn't a very charitable man."

"From what you've told me about him, that doesn't surprise me."

"I want to be free of him." Simon leaned his head back against the wall and closed his eyes for a moment, just breathing in the night air. The stuffiness of the attic was threatening to choke him. "That means free of his house. Free of his money. And free of his expectations."

"I noticed that you didn't say free of the car."

He opened his eyes and stared into her pretty blue ones. She made his heart skip a beat. He still couldn't believe that she was here with him. "That car is more mine than his anyway. At least, that's how I've always seen it."

"What you think you need to do to become free?" Merry dragged over another box of Christmas decorations. This one seemed filled with multicolored garland and nutcrackers.

"Definitely getting rid of the house and donating most of the money. Maybe I'll get a job working on a farm or a ranch. He would've hated that."

"Why?" Merry asked.

"Because he was a snob. He thought that blue-collar workers were beneath him. He would have been thrilled if I'd decided to become a lawyer or if I'd gone for a business degree. Instead, I got a liberal arts degree in prison. I hadn't planned on going for my bachelor's, but there wasn't much else I could do behind bars to keep myself sane."

She got up from the chair and gave him a hug. He hadn't realized how much he had needed that until he held her in his arms. She smelled like sunshine and he never wanted to let her go.

"Let's finish this up," he said, stepping back. Turning to the box she had been looking at, she sat down. "Do you remember any of these ornaments?"

"A few." Crouching next to her, he handed her a God's-eye wall hanging that he'd made out of Popsicle sticks and red and green yarn. "This work of art was done by yours truly, circa the middle school years."

"I think we've got three of those in our house as well. It was a good craft. It kept all of us quiet for about twenty minutes."

"I'll take these boxes downstairs too."

Merry followed him down, carrying the last of the Christmas boxes.

"You didn't tell me what Christmas miracle you're looking for," he said.

"I'm asking Santa to grant me first place in bronc busting, over LeAnn Keller."

"In the charity rodeo?"

"I wouldn't turn that down, but no. I need to do it during the next rodeo season. I want to win the all-around and get a belt in every category. But most of all, I need to get the belt for bronc riding. I'll go down in history as the first woman to buckle in that category. After that, I can retire."

"You can retire anytime you want."

"I want to retire with money in the bank and my credit cards paid off. Otherwise, I'm going to work too hard with too long hours trying to make ends meet. That's not what I want my future to look like."

"If you need money, I can loan you some." Bank of Braxton Reynolds could serve another purpose.

Merry shook her head. "I stopped taking charity a long time ago."

"It wouldn't be charity. It would be an interest-free loan."

She started to unbutton his shirt. "I don't need another bill to pay off."

"But—" he started to say.

She cut him off with a kiss that made him forget about bills, money, and Christmas miracles. He had the best miracle already—having her in his arms.

Chapter Fourteen

MERRY WAS SICK of talking about the future. She wanted right now to be special. And right now, Simon was in front of her with his delicious kisses and his strong arms. She didn't know if she would have a special birthday and Christmas in Last Stand that would rival Tahiti, but tonight could be magical, simply because she was with him.

"You know, I might have strained something carrying those boxes," she said, continuing to unbutton his shirt.

"I might be able to help rub out some of the aches and pains," he said, lifting her T-shirt over her head.

Grabbing him by the waistband of his jeans, she tugged him toward the hot tub on the porch. While he turned on the heater and the bubble jets, Merry stripped down and then walked back into the house to get a pitcher of sweet iced tea.

"I'm planning on working up a thirst," she said, bringing it back, along with two glasses filled with ice. She set it on the table next to the tub.

"I could get used to this," he said. "I love watching you walk around naked."

Merry twirled around, showing off. She craved the way his eyes darkened when they looked at her. Easing into the hot water, she sighed and positioned herself so the pulsating jets massaged her aching shoulder.

When he got into the tub with her, Simon pulled her onto his lap. His erection pressed against her hip as she held him close to her. The coarse hairs on his chest rubbed against her nipples when she leaned closer, seeking his mouth.

She could kiss him like this forever. His mouth tasted sweet and when his hand moved between her thighs, she opened them wide. Simon played with her until she was gasping and clinging to him. He kissed her deeply, not releasing her mouth until she cried out in pleasure. Relentlessly, Simon's fingers rubbed over her. Needing more, Merry shook and shivered. Kissing his neck, she bit down and sucked as he brought her over the edge.

"Simon," she moaned, tingles flowing up and down her body.

Turning to face him, Merry straddled his lap, then guided him inside her. Gripping his shoulders, she let the buoyancy of the water move her up and down on him. He held her still, though. Every thick inch of him filled her and she thought she would go mad if he didn't move.

Bending his head, he took one of her nipples in his mouth. After swirling his tongue around it and then sucking gently, Simon then repeated it with her other nipple.

"Oh yeah," she groaned, squeezing him tight.

His fingers dug into her ass to keep her from bouncing up and down on him like she wanted. Still, he kept up the wet tugging until her breasts were ultra-sensitive. Holding his head to them, she encouraged him to go harder.

"Please," she whispered.

With a hard suck that had her dancing over the edge of pleasure, Simon lifted them both out of the tub. Free to have him any way she wanted, Merry rode him while he bucked like a wild green. Only this ride wasn't going to end in injury. Running her hands down his chest, she admired the way his muscles tensed and shivered at her touch.

She found the rhythm to drive them both wild and when he gently smacked her ass, she came. Breathing hard, her thighs quivering and her entire body pulsing with a buzz of sheer pleasure, Merry leaned down and kissed him. Tangling her tongue with his, she let the aftershock of her orgasm shiver through her.

But Simon wasn't done with her. He slid out to put on a condom. She watched him guide the rubber over his hard cock, quivering in anticipation. Looking up at the Texas night sky, she felt like she was flying. And when he settled his mouth between her thighs, she gave herself up to the sensations. Watching the stars twinkling overhead, Merry felt every stroke of his tongue to her deepest core. She raised her hips up, eager for more as he licked her until she was wet and shaking.

"Please," she begged. "Fuck me now."

With a hungry growl, he kissed up her body until he got to her neck. He bit down on the soft flesh and sucked hard as he plunged inside of her again.

"Yes." Merry wrapped her legs around his waist as he

drove deep inside.

He made love to her hard and fast until the stars in the sky were just as bright when she closed her eyes to let her orgasm take over. Simon was breathing hard in her ear and the tickle of it was delicious.

"I can't get enough of you," he whispered.

"I'm not going anywhere," she said.

"You're everything I've ever wanted."

"Then take me."

It was effortless to rock with him as he chased his orgasm. Merry held on tight and kissed him roughly. His muscles tensed and he shouted in her mouth when he came. They kept moving, gradually slowing down, and then finally their bodies came to a rest. Panting and kissing, they eased back from each other.

"One of these days, I'm going to make love to you all night," he said. "Instead of having to rush back to the ranch." Simon threw out the condom while she slid back into the hot tub.

He poured them both a glass of iced tea and joined her in the tub.

"That'll be nice," she said. "How about Christmas Eve?"

Clinking glasses with her, he said, "It's a date."

Merry smiled and drank half of the glass in one big gulp. Having Simon under the Christmas tree—or at least next to it, by a roaring fireplace, was the Christmas fantasy she hadn't known she wanted, until right now.

THE NEXT MORNING, Merry wished she had been waking up next to Simon instead of in the bed-and-breakfast. But a quick look at the clock showed her that he was already up, had eaten breakfast hours ago, and was already working on repairing one of the fences on the Three Sisters Ranch.

Speaking of breakfast, she had better hurry downstairs because they stopped serving at ten thirty. After throwing on some clothes, she headed to the dining room. Luckily, there were still some hash browns left. She filled her plate with the last of the eggs and pancakes and the lone piece of bacon. A cup of coffee rounded out her breakfast and she found a quiet corner to eat.

As she was finishing up her meal, the owner of the Last Stand Bed-and-Breakfast came up to her.

"How's everything been?" Brenda McMann asked.

"Top notch," Merry said.

"I'm so glad. Were you planning on staying with us for another week?"

Merry hadn't thought that far ahead. But she didn't want to move back in with her mother just yet. "Sure." It was going to be a hit on her budget, but she was enjoying her privacy too much to care.

Brenda shifted uncomfortably. "We've been having trouble getting your card to go through. Do you happen to have another one we could use?"

Alarm flared through Merry. "Of course," she said through numbed lips. Did she? She'd have to check the balances. "I'll go get it after I finish here."

"There's no hurry." Brenda looked relieved and Merry

felt a pang of fear that she might have maxed out her card. "Thank you and enjoy the rest of your day."

Not likely, Merry thought. No longer hungry, she bussed her tray and hurried back to her room. She spent the next half hour juggling her credit cards around and begging one bank for a credit limit increase. After a tense few minutes, she was approved.

She had enough for another week at the bed-and-breakfast, and to pick up a few Christmas presents. But after that, she was on borrowed time. She was going to have to find a part-time job for January while she earned enough to get her and Raphael on the road again.

And then she had to start winning events in February, so she could have a steady stream of income coming in again.

After settling up with Brenda, Merry drove to the Three Sisters Ranch and went looking for Janice. She found her at the dressage ring that was adjacent to the retreat center. She was giving her horse Black Dahlia some exercise.

"You already charged my card for Raphael, right?" Merry asked when Janice was done with the exercise.

"Yeah, last month. Why?"

"Just making sure my card didn't decline. I'm having problems with it," Merry said.

"Computers are the worst, aren't they?" Janice said, shaking her head.

No, having your cards maxed out was the worst, but Merry let that slide for now. "I'm looking for something to do to keep busy until the circuit starts up again in February. Have you heard of anything?"

Janice tilted her head and stared off into space for a moment. "Nothing comes to mind, but I'll keep an ear out."

"Thanks."

"Are you going to board Raphael for January too?" she asked.

"Nah, Tulip misses him. I'm going to take him back home."

Nodding, Janice said, "We're going to miss him too. He's a big hit with everyone."

"He's a good horse," Merry said. "I'm going to go for a ride. Do you want to come with me?"

"I'd love to, but I've got to get back to work. If you're going to go trail riding, stay off the blue and red trails. The hogs are being more of a nuisance than normal."

"Will do," Merry said.

"How's the training going?" Janice asked.

"Good. I'll be ready for Saturday. How many tickets have you sold?"

"Enough to make a lot of families very happy."

That made all of this worth it. Some of the anxiety left her as they walked to the barn where Raphael was being boarded.

"Oh, I meant to ask you," Janice said. "What type of merch are you going to be selling?"

"Merch?" Merry asked.

"Yeah, I figured you and June would have your mom and April sell some souvenirs to the fans."

"That's allowed?" Merry asked.

"You need to pay for oats and gas somehow, right?"

This could be just the financial break she was looking for. Unfortunately, Merry didn't have a clue what she could sell. "Will LeAnn have a table?"

"Of course. You should see the setup the Kellers have planned. They're selling T-shirts, autographed pictures, key chains, the whole nine yards." Janice shook her head. "But I guess that's what it takes."

Merry and June never had done anything like that. Now seemed like a good time to start.

"I'll let you know by tomorrow."

"Sounds great. Have a nice ride." Janice patted her on the back and headed toward her retreat center.

Merry called June and left her a message when she didn't pick up. "We can sell stuff at the rodeo. Let's get together and figure out what we can come up with on short notice."

Then she called April, who thankfully picked up on the first ring.

"Hey, I need your help," Merry said and relayed to her what Janice had said.

"I wish I knew about this earlier," April said. "I could have done a risk assessment and done a profit and loss spreadsheet."

"That sounds like a lot of fun."

"It would have been." April totally missed the sarcasm.

"We'll do better next time. What can we do now? I'd like for us to clear a thousand dollars each." That would give her some breathing room with her finances until the circuit started back up in February. All this did was prove to her that she needed to have a plan before she quit the rodeo for how she was going to continue to make money when she wasn't competing anymore.

"That's ambitious," April said. "But let me do some market research. I think your best bet is to sell autographed pictures."

"What about T-shirts?" Merry asked. "LeAnn's doing that."

"That depends on whether we can get them printed in time. What's your budget?"

"Budget?"

"Damn it, Merry," April groaned.

"Not much."

"I'll see what I can do. But headshots of you and June are the first thing *you* should do. I'll call Kelly Sullivan and see if she can fit you in for a sitting. Free up your schedule."

"I'm wide open. Do you think we could do a Christmas pose instead of a head shot?"

"It's up to you, but you probably should get something that you could use year-round."

"Yeah, but I think a Christmas-themed picture would fit into the theme of the rodeo."

"That's for you and Kelly to decide. Let me know when you have the shots that you want and I'll price out how many to print and what we can sell them for to maximize profits."

"I knew I could count on you," Merry said.

"You should call Mom."

That was the last thing that she wanted to do. "Has she calmed down?"

"I think she's feeling bad about what she did."

"Good. She should."

"Merry, be nice."

"I will. Later. I'm going to go for a ride on Raphael now, and then I'll call her."

"I think you'll both feel better if you do."

Except Merry was still pissed off at her mother for how she'd treated Simon.

When she went to the barn, at least Raphael was happy to see her. Athena came over to say hello as she was saddling him up.

"Where's June?" she asked the horse.

Athena snorted and shook her head.

"Any ideas on how I can get Mama to treat Simon better?"

Athena didn't have an answer for that one.

Yeah, Merry didn't have one either. She didn't like how they had ended their conversation yesterday. Maybe now that Mama had gotten all that poison off her chest, had a good night's sleep and some holiday cheer from the parade and the tree lighting, they could move on.

She hoped.

Chapter Fifteen

M ERRY FELT BAD that on Simon's day off this week, he was stuck with her family. Even though it was for a good cause, the awkwardness still hadn't worn off and they were on their third store.

"What's on the list?" her mother asked, deliberately not looking at Simon.

"Nail polish and blue jeans, size twelve," he said.

June picked out several colors of polish, while April got the jeans.

Checking that off the list, her mother moved on while she pushed one of their three carriages along. So far, Penny hadn't apologized. But she also hadn't started in on Simon again.

"Next," her mother called out in drill-sergeant fashion.

"A jewelry-making kit."

"We need to go to a craft store for that."

Merry bit her lip when Simon barely managed to stifle a groan. Rising up on her tiptoes, she whispered in his ear, "I forgot to tell you that there's a long blow job in it for you after this."

Coughing, Simon wouldn't meet her mother's eye when

she turned to glare at him. "Next?"

"Cowboy boots, size nine, and rubber heel spur straps."

"I'm on it," June said.

"Next," her mother barked out.

"A deck of Magic: The Gathering cards, and a set of dice."

"I know where that is," April said.

That left the three of them alone. "Don't you dare leave me," he muttered to her.

"Never," she said, slipping her hand in his.

"Next!"

"That's all," Simon said, exhaling in relief.

"Hmmm," her mother said, wheeling the cart toward the front of the store. "Let's get in line."

"We'll be right with you," Merry said.

Her mother didn't bother to answer.

"I'm sorry she's being so rude." Merry squeezed his hand.

"It's all right. She'll either get used to me, or she won't."

"Do we have everything we need to clean up the cabin?" she asked as they passed by the home goods aisle.

"I'm set with garbage bags and cleaning supplies. Are you sure you want to spend our time doing chores?"

"Definitely. I want to work now so we can play later. And by playing, I mean having wild monkey sex."

"If you insist. What about practice time? Are you ready for the rodeo this week?"

"As ready as I'm going to be." She was staying on Tweety Pie longer, and her form was improving. But LeAnn was better. And that really sucked, considering February was getting closer.

"You'll do great. Nate told us that it's sold out."

Merry could only hope that a fraction of the ticket holders bought an autographed picture. They were selling them for twenty-five dollars each, which meant she had to sell forty to break even and eighty to turn the profit she wanted. She had one picture where she was dressed up in a sexy Mrs. Claus outfit, and then another that was more her, where she was wearing jeans and a T-shirt with the Texas flag as a backdrop. The third picture was of her and Raphael going around the barrels. The action shot had been her favorite, even though Kelly did a fantastic job on all of them. June had one of her roping a calf as her action shot, and then just a standard head shot.

April was going to watch LeAnn's sales like a hawk to see if it was worth selling T-shirts as well. June wanted to sell hats that had "Bad Reputation" stitched on them, but no one could make them in time for this event.

Merry tossed a set of Christmas lights in the shape of cowboy boots into the carriage. "For luck," she said.

They caught up with her mother and sisters, who dumped the presents they'd found into the carriages. It took a while for the cashier to check them out. When Simon put everything on his credit card, Merry winced at the total. But it went through without a problem.

"We're going back home to wrap," June said.

"But we're going to need the list," her mother said, holding out her hand, but still not looking at Simon.

"I really appreciate this," Simon said. "Thank you."

Her mother's posture softened. And Merry knew that progress was being made, even though it was going too slow for her liking.

"You're welcome," her mother said grudgingly. "It's a nice thing that you're doing."

But she still didn't apologize.

Merry's heart sank.

Her sisters went with their mother. She watched them drive out of the parking lot, wondering if she could have said or done something different.

She was trying not to let it bother her, but she felt herself growing more and more melancholy as they drove to the cabin. Merry had forgotten how out of the way it was, but when she caught her first sight of it in ten years, her heart pounded like it was the first time.

It was a log cabin and it resembled the houses she used to build with Lincoln Logs when she was a kid.

"We should have gotten a wreath for the door," she murmured, when they got out of the car and headed in.

"We will, once all the work is done. Brace yourself," Simon said, his hand on the door. "It's not as pretty as you remember."

He pushed open the door and then held it for her as she walked in. He was right. It had been neglected. There were cobwebs and sketchy-looking piles of what Merry hoped was dirt, though her nose was telling her it was probably something else.

"I've got gloves and masks in the kitchen. At least they've got the lights on." Simon flicked the switch.

The cabin looked worse under the bright lights.

"Having second thoughts?" he asked.

She shook her head. "Nope. Let's get started."

Merry started on the kitchen while Simon worked on the large living room. As she swept and scrubbed, she was happy to see that the dirt, dust, and grime hadn't done any real damage. And after a few hours and many buckets of soap and water, Merry was exhausted, but pleased at putting a dent into the work needed to make the little kitchen shine.

She was sitting down at the table, wondering how Simon was going to decorate the kitchen when he staggered in and slumped into a chair.

"That's it for me," he said. "The contractors finished this floor, but they hit a snag in the upstairs. I wanted them to put in central air but they've got to do some rewiring. And the bathrooms need some work as well."

"Are you going to flip the cabin?" she asked.

"I don't know," he said. "I haven't given myself the time to think about it. I'll probably live here for a while though, after the retreat is over. But I don't know how long I'll be staying. That's part of the reason your mom is so pissed at me. She thinks I'm going to abandon you."

"I'd like to see you try," Merry said with a sad smile. She didn't have the heart to tell him that she was afraid he would, too.

"Anyway, I was hoping that after the rodeo, we could decorate for Christmas."

"I'd like that," Merry said. "Is the fireplace usable?"

Simon shrugged. "I'll add it to the contractor's list of

things to do."

"It's not important. The nights haven't been chilly. It's just something that I've always wanted to have going, while we decorated for Christmas."

"Consider it done."

"You don't have to," she said.

"It'll be my birthday present to you."

She smiled, her heart melting into a pile of goo. He was going to break her heart if she wasn't careful. "We should go grab some dinner and lots of coffee and then come back here and put in a few more hours."

"Might as well," he said. "I had great plans to seduce you in the living room, but I don't think the floors and walls are ready for us."

"Not to mention, I don't think I'd be able to keep my eyes open for very long." She stifled a yawn.

"You can close your eyes," he said. "I don't mind."

She leaned in to kiss him. His mouth was warm and welcoming. "We should put on some Christmas carols while we work," she said when they came up for air. Part of her wanted to convince him to take her back to his father's place where they could soak in the hot tub and then roll around on soft cotton sheets on a big king-sized bed. But that wouldn't get the cabin ready for Simon to live in. And if he didn't have a place to stay once the retreat was over, he might leave.

And Merry wasn't ready to say goodbye yet.

SIMON FELL FACE-FIRST into his bed at the retreat center. Four a.m. was going to come real fast, but even though he was physically spent, his mind was racing. Christmas had never been special for him. At best, it had been opening up lots of presents when he was a kid. At worst, it had been an ordeal to endure after his parents had divorced.

Rolling over, Simon tried not to wake Chris as he fumbled for the packet that the banker had given to him. He knew there was nothing in it that could possibly make up for ten years of prison. And he really didn't want to open it. Maybe he could give it to Charlie to look at, to make sure that there wasn't anything of value inside.

That seemed cowardly though. If Simon wanted to know what was in it, he should open it himself. But he was afraid that if he did, he would never be free of his father and the ugliness of his father's life. Simon lay on his back and stared up at the ceiling.

The cabin had always been a place of good memories. First with his mother, before the drinking began. His father had thought the place was too remote and rustic, and he'd preferred to stay home when she and Simon would come out on weekends. He knew now that it had just been an excuse, that his father had been using that time to be with his girlfriends. But he hadn't cared—he hadn't missed his father's presence at all. He and his mother would go riding during the day and play board games at night. And they would listen to the radio when the television reception was on the fritz.

After the divorce, his mother didn't go out to the cabin

anymore. She preferred to stay closer to the cities and the society parties. At that point, Simon came out alone or with friends, and eventually Merry. He should have taken her to the cabin that night instead of his father's house. But it had been her birthday, and he had wanted to show off.

Regrets washed over him, leaving him even more unable to sleep.

Why hadn't he bent his stubborn neck and begged his father not to press charges?

Because he couldn't. Probably for the same reason, he couldn't open that letter now. He didn't want to give the son of a bitch the satisfaction. He shot up out of bed and brought the letter into the bathroom with him. After ripping open the envelope, he dumped the paper in the sink. It looked like a letter. No stock certificates. No bonds. No cash. Simon tore the papers into strips, refusing to read a word. He shredded the strips into confetti, then scooped the mess into the trash can.

By the time he was done, he was breathing heavily. It had been harder than he'd thought not to read the words. But the sight of his father's scrawled handwriting had turned his stomach. Simon had been right. The package had contained the last words of a dying man trying to explain himself.

Fuck that noise.

Braxton didn't get to control him from beyond the grave. He couldn't force Simon to read his words.

Maybe he needed to get out of Texas…if only to see if his father's specter would still haunt him, even if he was far away.

But then he'd be leaving Merry, and he wasn't sure if the chance of finding peace would be worth sacrificing what they'd rekindled. He hoped in his heart, though, for one nice Christmas memory with her. One that if his life exploded in a fiery mess of emotions and crap, he could think back on and hold close to his heart. He'd add it to the scrapbook of memories he had with her. Because who was he kidding? He wasn't any good for her. He wasn't even good for himself. Punching his pillow, Simon flopped on his stomach and willed himself to sleep.

Chapter Sixteen

MERRY LIVED FOR rodeo days. She would never take for granted the excitement of the crowd or the sheer pleasure of seeing families come together and cheer for their favorite athletes, both the two- and four-legged ones.

April and their mother had set themselves up on vendor row. April was in charge of scheduling the autograph sessions for Merry and June, and Mama was in charge of the money. They might not be the well-oiled machine that the Keller family was, but they made it work. Things were still a little chilly between her and her mother, but Merry was trying not to dwell on that.

"You ready to take second place in barrel racing?" June asked.

"Pride goes before the fall," Merry replied as she and Raphael headed to their mark. She was one of the first riders, while June was in the middle of the pack.

"Try not to fall off of Raphael," June joked.

Merry flipped her off. There were a few gasps and she wondered if she'd be a meme later on. She hoped so.

"I'll be in the stands trying to take some video to put on Instagram," June said.

"Just don't be late for your own turn," Merry quipped.

"Yes, Mom," June droned. "Like I haven't done this before."

"Whatever," Merry said. "Just make sure to get my good side."

"That'll be hard, considering you're sitting on it."

"Next up is Merry Grayson from Last Stand, Texas," the announcer said.

The crowd went wild. Merry waved to them as she guided Raphael to the chute.

Merry nudged Raphael and they flew down the straightaway. The sounds of the crowd faded away as they circled around the first barrel. They were in good position and whipped around the second barrel. Damn, she loved this horse. He moved like the wind. She urged him around the third.

"That horse has got the juice," the announcer said.

"Get 'em boy," she said as they cleared the third barrel and raced back in.

That's when something went wrong. She felt Raphael slip. Heard the snap.

"No," Merry screamed and leapt off him, landing hard. Her ankle buckled, but she ignored the sharp pain.

"Fourteen-oh-seven," the announcer said.

"Get Janice," she sobbed.

Luis and Bob, two of the Three Sisters Ranch hands who were helping out at the rodeo today took Raphael's reins and gently led him out of the busy area. Merry limped after them, looking for June. She didn't see her.

She grabbed the next cowboy she recognized, another of the ranch hands. "Frenchie," she said. "Don't let June know Raphael's hurt. Not until after her ride."

"You're hurt," he said, giving her a steady arm.

"I'm fine." Merry winced, but she had to get to the barn where they would have taken Raphael. "Did they call Janice or Honeyman?"

Janice was a vet tech and the Honeyman family ran the veterinarian hospital in Last Stand.

Frenchie asked the question into his walkie-talkie. An unfamiliar voice buzzed back. "Janice is on her way. Reba Keller is with the horse now."

"Good," Merry gasped and staggered faster.

Janice had beaten her there. Both she and Reba were in the stall with Raphael.

"How is he?" Merry asked, leaning against the stall door for support.

Simon came into the barn at a full run. "I got this from here," Simon said to Frenchie.

Merry welcomed his arms around her and sagged against his strength.

"It's a break or a fracture," Reba said. "I won't know without X-rays."

Merry whimpered.

"We've given him a tranquilizer and something for the pain," Janice said. "Seth Honeyman is bringing the portable unit."

Reba looked up and saw Merry's stricken face. "He's going to heal from this."

Merry nodded.

Janice frowned at Reba.

"I know he's not going to be able to race again," Merry said in a small voice. She was proud that her voice didn't shake. She owed it to Simon's strong grip. "I don't care about that. He just has to be okay. That's all I care about." The tears threatened, but Simon held her tighter. She'd be able to get through this, as long as he didn't let go.

"While we work on Raphael, you need to get that ankle wrapped."

"I'm fine," she said, but then she put weight on it. "Or maybe not."

Simon scooped her up like she weighed nothing.

"Don't take me to the first aid tent," Merry said, clinging to him.

"Take her into the rodeo school." Janice tossed him a set of keys. "I'll send an EMT in."

"I can wrap it myself," Merry protested.

"But you're not going to." Simon carried her away. She craned her neck, keeping Raphael in her sight as long as she could.

"What the fuck am I going to do now?" Merry whispered.

﹌

AFTER HER ANKLE was taped up, Merry limped back to Raphael's side. June had met her halfway and crushed her with a hug.

"He's going to be okay," Merry said. It had to be just a fracture, not a break. A fracture would heal. A break was risky. Keeping a horse immobile for the bone to heal was almost impossible. Her brain refused to go to what the next step might be after that.

"What happened?" June asked.

"I'm not sure. He slipped in the dirt. I heard a snap." Merry took a shaky breath.

June gripped her hand and with Simon on the other side of her, supporting her, they went back to Raphael.

"It's a star fracture," Reba said as soon as she saw them.

Janice hurried over to hug Merry. Merry couldn't stop the tears and sobbed in relief.

"What's that mean?" Simon asked.

"It means there are multiple cracks in the bone," Seth Honeyman said, packing up the X-ray unit. "And while it's painful at first, the pain will resolve quickly and with proper treatment, it should completely heal."

"There's your Christmas miracle, baby," Simon said and kissed her on the head.

Merry nodded, wiping her eyes.

"Thanks," she said.

"He's resting now," Seth said. "And he isn't in pain. I'll be back later to check on him and go over care. He's got a splint and bandage on him now, but I'd like to put a plaster cast on him tomorrow."

"Whatever you suggest. Thank you," she said, resisting the urge to hug him as well.

"We've got to get back," Janice said. "But you have my

number. Call if you need me."

"I will. Thank you all so much," she said. "Reba, I truly appreciate you being here so fast." Merry held out her hand to shake it, but Reba tugged her into a hug.

"I was glad to be here."

The hug felt good and shored her up a bit. Merry had a feeling that she was going to need a lot more hugs.

After Reba left, Merry asked, "Can you give me some time alone with him?"

"You got it." June gave her another rib-crushing hug.

"Sure," Simon said. "Just let me get a chair."

After June left, Simon kissed her again and made sure she was steady and braced on the stall door before leaving her. He came back with an office chair that looked out of place in the barn, but she was grateful for the back support.

"I'll be close by. Give a shout when you're ready to go."

"I'm fine. The ankle is starting to feel better." Or maybe the over-the-counter pain medicine she took was starting to kick in.

With a final hug, Simon reluctantly left her alone with her horse.

"I'm so sorry," she said, breaking down. Reaching into the stall, she stroked his nose lovingly. "We should have quit last year. Before broncs. You were ready. I was ready. I promise you, if you get better, you will live your best life. Or the best one you can with that little tyrant Tulip."

Raphael chuffed and his eyes closed.

"Get some rest, boy."

She wasn't sure how long she sat there, only that her

neck and back muscles were starting to cramp. Standing up, Merry experimentally rotated her ankle. It hurt, but in a more annoying way than actual pain. The swelling was down too. It was probably just a bad twist.

"There she is. There's my girl."

Merry looked up in disbelief. "Luke?" she said.

And like a dream, her father was striding toward her. She would have gone to him for a hug, but she noticed he had two little girls with him.

"What are you doing back here?" she asked.

"I asked one of the workers where you were," he said. "I told them I was your father."

Merry bit back a groan. The volunteers couldn't have known that he was using the term father rather loosely. She forced a smile. The last thing she wanted to do was promotional bullshit. But her fans had gotten her and Raphael this far. They owed them a smile and some time. "And who are these two young cowgirls?"

"They're your sisters, Betty and Lulu."

Shock froze Merry into place. "S-sisters?" she stuttered. They looked to be about ten years old. They had been born while she was in high school, while Simon was getting sentenced to prison. She had wondered where her father had been during her high school years. This answered the question. It was suddenly hard to breathe.

Turning back to Raphael, she blinked back tears. What was she going to say to them? How was she going to keep from yelling at her father?

"Hello," one of them said warily.

Suck it up, buttercup, she told herself.

"Hello," she said, turning around. Wincing, she crouched down and held out her hands for a hug. They almost knocked her over but she gamely held on. "Why am I just meeting them now?" She forced her voice to be light and polite. But she was furious at her father. Not at the girls, though.

"Can we have a picture with you and Raphael?" Betty—or was it Lulu?—asked.

Merry looked over her shoulder. Raphael poked his nose over the stall in curiosity. "Sure," she said.

"Good. We weren't going to pay twenty-five bucks for one," Luke said, bringing up his cell phone camera.

She was pretty sure her mother would have given him the photos for free. But she was equally sure that he hadn't wanted to approach her with Betty and Lulu in tow.

"Thank you," the girls chorused and then turned to their father. "Can we go find June now?"

"You betcha," he said and reached down to hold their hands. "We'll be rooting for you to take first place in the final barrel-racing run."

"Oh, I can't compete. Raphael got hurt on that last one."

"What?" her father said sternly. "I didn't raise you to be a quitter."

The fact that he thought he'd raised her at all was funny in a sad sort of way.

"I think you should go," Simon said from behind her.

"Simon," she said quietly. She hadn't known he was in earshot.

"I got this." He moved in front of her.

"Who the hell are you?" Luke blustered.

"I'm the one asking you to leave before you get yourself embarrassed in front of your daughters."

"Simon," Merry repeated, placing a hand on his shoulder.

"Are you going to let him talk to me that way?" Luke said.

"I'm not having a lot of luck stopping him," Merry said dryly.

"Your fans paid a lot of money to see you win. You need to find another horse and get back out there."

"This is the last time I'm asking you politely," Simon said, taking a threatening step forward.

"Come on, girls," Luke said and hurried out of the barn with them.

"He's right," Merry said, as much as she hated to admit it.

"It doesn't matter. You're hurt."

"I can finish the rodeo up." Merry sighed. "I've just got to find a horse."

"You don't have to do this," Simon said. "You can barely walk."

"I'm fine. Let's go see what Trent has for barrel-racing horses." She called April.

"We just heard about Raphael. I'm so sorry," April said. "Do you need us to come over there?"

"Thank you. No, I'm good. I've got to find another horse so I can do the next set."

"Wait, what? June said you were hurt too."

"No, I'm fine."

Simon scoffed, but he continued to walk her back to the rodeo school.

"Can you see if Cole or Trent can meet me at the barn where they keep the training horses. I'd like to borrow one."

"You're not going to win with those guys," April said. "Even I know that."

"I don't need to win," Merry said. "I just need to do a cloverleaf and wave to the crowd."

"If you're sure," April said.

"I need to do this. For me and for Raphael."

"All right then. I'll have Cole meet you. You won't have much time to do a practice run on a strange horse."

"Let me worry about that."

But when they hobbled back to the rodeo school, it wasn't Trent or Cole waiting for them. It was Kelly Sullivan. She was standing next to her roan.

"Are you good to ride?" Kelly asked.

Merry nodded. She'd be in a world of hurt later, but that was what ice and ibuprofen were for.

"This is Pippi. She was my barrel-racing horse. She's not a firecracker like Athena, Raphael or hell, even Emily's Sunflower. But she's solid and she knows what to do. I'd be honored if you rode her today."

Merry blinked back tears. "Thank you."

"I don't care if you take first place, but if you could beat Emily, I'd appreciate it."

Merry grinned, recognizing the friendly sibling rivalry. "I'll not only beat Emily, but I'll beat June, too."

Chapter Seventeen

AFTER THE RODEO, things slowed down to what the ranch hands called a normal pace. As Simon was heading out to his car after having dinner with the retreat members and the ranch hands, Luis ran up to him.

"Hey," he said. "I meant to tell you at dinner but I forgot. I have a friend who works on a cattle ranch in Harris County. He says they're looking to hire hands in January for part-time work. It's guaranteed until after calving season in the spring. The money isn't any great shakes, but it's a start. I can vouch for you if you're interested."

"Wow, that's great," Simon said. With the rodeo and Christmas coming up, he hadn't had a moment to think about his future—which was pretty dumb considering the retreat ended a few days before the end of the year. But Harris County, in Houston, was a long way away and things were still up in the air with Merry.

She had won the barrel-racing event, just barely beating June. If her first ride with Raphael hadn't been so good, she wouldn't have made it. For being on a new horse, though, Merry gave it her all. Simon would have been proud of her either way, but he was glad she was able to win in her category.

She sold a lot of autographs that day. She stayed until every single person in line got a chance to talk to her, whether they were buying a photo or not. Luckily, she had been reasonable and agreed to sit down with her ankle elevated with ice on it. She'd placed third in bronc busting and managed to stay on the horse for the full eight seconds. It had been tricky for her with her bum ankle to switch over to the pick-up horse, and she'd landed badly. But she hadn't done any more damage to it.

Simon hadn't seen a lot of her this week because she had been settling Raphael in at her mother's place and resting her ankle. But tonight, they were going to spend time together at the cabin. It wasn't perfect, but it would be enough for the two of them. He was even going to stay the night and get up hella early to drive back to the ranch to start the day.

"This is some car." Luis whistled. "You know, at first I didn't think I'd like you."

"Why's that?" Simon asked.

"You had this flashy car. You had your own house. And to add insult to injury, you're dating Merry Grayson."

"I can see how that would make me unpopular," he said.

"But you know your stuff. Don't think us guys haven't noticed that you never tried to pull the rich boy attitude on us."

"I'm not a rich boy," he said.

"You are from where I'm standing."

Simon supposed that was true.

"Anyway, don't forget us after spring comes around.

Things are looking up around the Three Sisters Ranch. There might be a full-time spot for you if you're interested."

Was he interested?

Merry was heading out on the circuit in February, concentrating solely on bronc busting. She was taking Tinkerbell with her, which made him wince every time he thought about it. Sure, she would always have roots in the town. But he didn't. He wasn't sure if what he needed was a complete break from his past or not. If that was the case, it meant putting Last Stand in his rearview mirror, leaving Merry behind. And he didn't want to do that. Not yet.

"Thanks, Luis." He shook his hand.

"Are you going to take Merry to the Jameson House charity ball this Wednesday?"

"Another charity event?"

"They're all over the place this time of the year."

"Sadly, I haven't received my invitation." He wasn't sad in the slightest.

"You don't need one. Charlie set it up so the retreat members get to go."

Simon stifled a groan. That figured. But Charlie needed to show off his hard work to people who were known donors, so he supposed he owed it to the man to be a part of the dog and pony show. "How formal is this formal?"

"You can get away with rodeo formal. I can let you borrow a bolo tie if you need it."

Simon wondered if Merry was up for another shopping trip. Maybe she'd let him buy her a sexy little black dress. He'd ask Charlie if he could bring Merry with him as his date, if she wasn't already going. There was no way Charlie would say no to Last Stand's darling of the rodeo coming along with his group.

"I'll let you know, but thanks for the offer."

"You guys will be there for the kids' party at the fire station on Christmas Eve, right?"

"I think so."

"It's a good time. I like seeing all the kids get so excited about the toys. Did you hear some big shot bought up all the Christmas wishes on the giving tree?"

"I hadn't heard that, no," Simon said, hiding a smile while he got into his car.

"That's my kind of party. Anyway, don't stay out too late. We've got an early day tomorrow and a long ride. We're not going to get back before sundown. You want to be well rested."

"I'll take that under advisement."

"Yeah, if I had Merry Grayson waiting for me, I wouldn't listen to that advice either. Have a good night." Luis gave him a half wave and jogged back to the ranch house.

Luis was a good guy, and Simon liked working with the other ranch hands. Maybe part of letting go of his father's influence was to stop thinking about the old man whenever he was about to make an important decision. What would his father think of him being a ranch hand in Last Stand?

Who gives a fuck?

That should be his answer. Instead, it was like he was still arguing with the old man. Maybe it would be better once the house was sold and he was far away and free. Houston suddenly didn't seem so bad.

And yet, the sight of Merry's truck outside of the cabin made his heart skip a beat in anticipation.

"It smells good in here," he said, for a moment picturing they were married and he was returning home from his job.

Of course, the fantasy only worked if Merry had a job that let her out early enough that she could cook dinner.

"I got takeout from The Hut this afternoon. I'm warming it up now."

With food from Hutchinson's BBQ Market, home-cooked meals weren't a priority. What was a priority was kissing Merry senseless. He backed her up against the wall, being careful of her ankle.

"I missed you today," he said when they came up for air.

"I've been waiting for you to come home," she said, linking her fingers behind his neck.

Home? Was that what this place was? He still didn't feel it, but he was willing to pretend. Home seemed to be where she was anyways.

"How's Raphael?"

"He's not happy, but he's going to make it. I'm moving out of the bed-and-breakfast, and back in with my mom and June so I can take care of him."

Simon kissed her again because she looked worried.

"The vet bills are going to kill me," she said. "But I made some money selling autographs at the rodeo, so maybe that will buy me some time on my credit cards until I can sell Tweety Pie."

He wasn't sorry that she was getting rid of that nightmare of a horse, but he knew Merry would miss not having a horse with her. "What about practicing?"

"I'm as good as I'm going to get. Having Tweety Pie is a luxury I can't afford right now."

"I know you shot me down the last time I offered, but…"

She placed a hand on his mouth. "No. I do this by myself or not at all."

He kissed her fingers. "Anyone ever tell you that you're stubborn?"

"No," she deadpanned.

"That's because no one's had the balls," he said. "I'm going to take a shower." He swatted her on the behind as he passed, and dodged the punch she threw at him in retaliation.

Grinning at her wildly and seeing the matching joy in her face, the words *I love you* were almost out of his mouth before he could swallow them back. Shocked, he whirled away and made a beeline to the bathroom. Under the hot, pulsating spray of the shower, he wondered just where the hell that thought had come from. And then he realized it had already been there, all along. Ever since the first moment he saw her riding barrels around on the high school's horse.

The question now was, what was he going to do about it?

Nothing could be done. She had her rodeo season ahead and he was going to be adrift in a few weeks. Maybe he'd get the job in Houston and maybe he wouldn't. Maybe the house would sell right away and maybe it wouldn't. There were too many maybes in his future. But at least she'd only be a phone call away.

After his shower, he got dressed and came back into the living room. He saw that Merry had set the table as if they were eating a fancy meal instead of barbecue. The doorbell rang, but before he could go to answer it, he heard Merry opening the door and talking with whomever was there.

"Who is it?" Simon asked.

"It's your step-monster," Merry said.

"Joyce?" Simon strode to the door and saw that Merry had already backed Joyce up off the porch and toward her car.

As much as he would've liked to see Merry menace Joyce, he didn't want any trouble.

"It's okay, Merry. I got this."

Merry crossed her arms and took a single step back, all the while glaring daggers at Joyce. Joyce looked scared, and perhaps she had every right to be. But Simon's beef had never really been with Joyce. His father had done them both wrong. There was no sense in keeping the animosity alive. Joyce was nothing to him, and he was nothing to her, either.

"Why are you here?" Simon said. "I thought I made it clear in my last message that anything you needed from my father's estate you can get through his lawyers."

"If you had just picked up, we could have done this over the phone and I wouldn't have had to come out all this way and bother you at home."

Home. There was that word again.

"What was so important that you had to track me

down?"

Reaching into her large handbag, Joyce pulled out a familiar-looking padded envelope. Simon had a sinking feeling in his stomach that he knew exactly what that was.

"I get $10,000 if I deliver this to you. All I have to do is take a picture of you holding it in order for me to get my money."

"What is it?" Merry asked her suspiciously.

"It's a letter from his father. He wanted to make sure that Simon received this."

"Do you know what it says?" he asked.

"Not a clue."

Simon didn't reach for it. "You get paid just for delivering it, right?"

"Yeah." She pulled out her phone. "I hand you a letter. I take a snapshot of you holding it up. I send it to the lawyer. He transfers ten grand into my bank account."

"So you get paid whether I read it or not?" He couldn't believe this shit. Wait, yes he could. This was Braxton Reynolds trying to manipulate him from beyond the grave again.

"I don't care if you use it for toilet paper. I just want my money."

"You want his father's money," Merry said.

Joyce shrugged. "Yeah, whatever."

It didn't matter to him if Joyce got the money or not. It was a simple enough thing he could do for her. "Fine, give it to me."

Eagerly, Joyce handed him the envelope. "Okay," she

said. "Hold it up to your face."

Feeling foolish, he did.

Joyce snapped a couple of pictures. "Let me make sure it goes through."

Simon looked at the envelope and hefted the weight in his hand. It felt as thick as the other letters had been. He wondered how many of these packages his father had sent around. He hoped this was the last one.

"Confirmed," Joyce chirped. "Thank you, Simon, I really appreciate it." She looked conflicted for a moment, but then straightened her shoulders and looked him in the eye. "I'm sorry I made you feel uncomfortable all those years ago. I had wanted to hurt your father, but I never intended to hurt you, too. I'm sorry."

Maybe there was something about Christmas being a time for miracles after all. "I don't bear you any ill will, Joyce. Have a good life," Simon said before he got choked up.

"Go on get," Merry said, making shooing gestures with her hands.

It tickled him that Merry held a grudge on his behalf, even when he no longer cared. After getting into her car, Joyce pulled away.

Simon went to rip up the package, but Merry stopped him by grabbing it.

"What are you doing?" he asked.

"Whoa," she said. "That's your dad's last words to you."

"So?" Simon said, pulling the packet away from her.

"You can't just rip it up without reading it."

"Why not? It's what I've done with all of his letters. I've got no desire to read the words of a dying man seeking absolution for his sins—if that's even what's in here. He knew what he did to me. And he wasn't sorry for it until he started dying. I don't need for him to get the last word in my life. As far as I'm concerned, the last thing he said to me was: *This will teach you, boy.*"

"Wouldn't it be satisfying to hear his apology, though? Wouldn't that give you closure?"

"I've got his car, his house, and just gave his ex-wife ten grand. I'd say everything is pretty much closed." He went to rip it up again.

Merry snatched it out of his hand. "I'm not going to let you do this."

"Merry, it's my letter. Give it back to me." He attempted to grab it, but she stepped away and held it behind her back.

"Don't play games with me about this. Give me the letter, so I can destroy it and we can get on with the nice evening you had planned." Anger was edging into him, and he tried to push aside those feelings. He just wanted to have a nice dinner with her with wine, candlelight, and romance. Not to mention having mind-blowing sex, cuddling for a bit, and falling asleep in her arms before he had to go back to the retreat center, so he could be a functioning human being at four in the morning. He literally did not have time for this bullshit. It pissed him off that his father was ruining this for him, just like he ruined everything good in his life.

"You're going to regret it for the rest of your life if you destroy this letter."

He didn't want to do this. He didn't want to deal with Braxton or his bullshit. He was having a hard enough time trying to figure out what his life was going to be like. He was exhausted from riding all day and fixing up the cabin all night. He needed a break. He needed to relax. He didn't need this shit.

"No, I won't. It's going in the fire. Please, give it back to me or we're going to have a problem."

That was obviously the wrong thing to say because Merry's head reared back as if he had hit her. "I'm trying to help you."

"If you want to help, you'd listen to what I'm telling you. I want nothing to do with the man. He was the prick who shot at you. Don't you remember?"

"I never got a chance to meet him," Merry said. "Maybe he mellowed out in his old age."

Simon snorted. "Fat chance. He wouldn't have wanted to meet you. He would've thought you weren't good enough for me. He would have judged you because your family lived in a trailer instead of a house. He was an insensitive jerk and he would've hurt your feelings just because it made him feel superior. He was a man who always wanted to get the last word and always wanted to win, no matter the cost—even when that cost was his son. The context of that letter—" Simon pointed at her angrily "—is proof positive that he isn't really sorry for what he did. Otherwise, he would've respected my wishes and left me alone. If he truly wanted to make amends, that's what he would've done."

"I don't see it that way," she said.

"You don't have to. All you have to do is give me that letter."

"People have regrets. Do you know what I would give to have my father tell me that he was sorry for abandoning me and my sisters for his new family?"

"He didn't look sorry, Merry. In fact, he looked like he was happy with his decision."

She blew out a breath, as if he had punched her in the stomach.

"Please, Merry." He held out his hand. "I hate fighting. I'm at the end of my rope here. I know what I'm doing. I've dealt with this type of shit from him before. Please give me the letter."

"What would you give to hear him tell you how sorry he was? How much he regretted doing what he did?"

"It's not worth it. Because chances are, all you're holding is a letter that justifies him acting like a prick and trying to run my life from beyond the grave."

She shook her head. "If you're just going to destroy it anyway, let me keep it. That way if you ever change your mind, you can open it."

"I won't change my mind." He sighed. He couldn't take much more of this. "Merry, you have to understand… I need to put him behind me. I need to take away his power over me. Destroying the letter will do that."

"No." She shook her head. "If you destroy this letter unread, he wins."

"How?"

"Because you still give a shit about what he says. If you

didn't, the letter wouldn't hold this much power over you."

That stung. Her words pierced him. "He is nothing to me," he said between his teeth. But that letter could have the power to change everything and he didn't want anything to be changed. He didn't want to risk that for some unknown reason he might forgive his father. He didn't want to risk that the letter condemned Simon for every bad thing that ever happened to Braxton.

"He's your father," she said. "He's also an asshole. But if you destroy this letter, you will always wonder what he wanted you to know so badly that he spent ten grand to have it delivered."

"You didn't know him. I did. Ten grand was nothing for him."

"Don't let him control you," she said.

"He killed my mother," Simon cried out in anguish, the pain searing through him.

"No, he didn't. From what you've told me, she was an alcoholic."

"Because of him," he snarled.

"Was it?"

"Let's not talk about mothers," Simon warned.

"Hey, both your mom and mine did the best they could with what they had. They were flawed. We're all flawed."

"I can't do this, right now," he said. "I'm exhausted. Give me the packet. You have no right to take it. It's my property."

Merry started backing away toward her truck.

He had to stop her. "Merry, if you do this, we're

through."

That stopped her in her tracks all right. "What?"

"That's how serious I am right now." But when he took a step forward, she took a step back. "Don't do this to us."

"Us," she said, her voice high and shaky. "There's not much of 'us' if this is what it takes to end things."

"Just give me the letter and we can pretend that this never happened."

"I don't pretend very well."

That was when he lost his temper. "I get that you have Daddy issues. You handle them your way. I'll handle mine my way."

"You bastard," she said through clenched teeth.

"This isn't about me and my father. You just said it yourself. You would give everything to have your father apologize for abandoning you. Newsflash—he never will."

"Go to hell," she said, turning and running for her truck.

"Just like my father would never apologize." He could have caught up to her. She had a bum ankle, but all he could do was watch her go. She was crying and swearing at him. After slamming the door, she put the truck into gear and tore out of the driveway and out of his life.

Maybe this was for the best. For both of them. But it felt like shit.

Chapter Eighteen

MERRY HID HER misery under several coats of mascara and the brightest lipstick she could find. She threw herself into taking care of the horses and dodging her mother's questions about Simon. She got lucky in that June and April were spending more time with Cole and Esteban than they were with her and her mother. She didn't want to talk about Simon and rehash what had happened between them. She knew she'd have to talk about it sooner or later, but Merry wanted to wait until the pain was more manageable. Right now, she felt like she had a star fracture in her heart. It would ease, but it was taking its sweet time.

She met up with her sisters in the Kellers' spacious Winnebago for the interview that Dolly had set up.

"Welcome," Dolly said, gesturing her to sit on the couch with April and June. They each had a fruity-looking cocktail in their hand and a plate of mini quiches. "Can I get you a drink?"

"Whiskey, neat," she said, flopping down on the couch. She popped a quiche in her mouth from off of June's plate. It was warm and flaky, and if Merry had been alone, she would have commandeered the entire platter.

"Hey," June snapped.

Dolly staved off a food fight by filling up everyone's plate again and leaving the tray on the coffee table in front of them. Then she handed her three fingers of whiskey. Merry smirked. This was going to be one hell of an interview. She had a few more quiches to coat her stomach, even though she wanted to down the whole glass to drown out the emptiness she felt.

"How's your ankle doing?" Dolly asked.

"Almost good as new," Merry said. It still gave her twinges when she had been on her feet too long, but Merry welcomed the distraction from the ache in her heart.

She wished Simon hadn't broken up with her. Didn't he know that every man in her life had looked for an excuse to leave her? Merry had hoped that he would have been different. She could have sworn he was. But at their first major disagreement, he'd tossed her to the curb. It hurt that he had been so cruel when all she was trying to do was help.

"And Raphael is settled in?"

"Yeah," Merry said. "He's never going to barrel race again, but Seth Honeyman—the best vet in this area—thinks he'll live a normal life."

"I'm so glad. A lot of your fans have been worried about him."

"I've been getting letters," Merry said.

"So…April," Dolly said, turning in her chair to look at her. "Why didn't you get into rodeo like your sisters?"

"I had an incident growing up that made me afraid of horses. I've been working on it, but I still don't like them."

"Not even Raphael and Athena?" Dolly teased.

Merry and June shot April a look, but April ignored them. "Especially not them. They're spoiled prima donnas." But she said the words with a smile, so Merry didn't feel the need to smush a quiche in her face.

"Was it hard living in your sisters' shadow?"

April scoffed. "No way. If it wasn't for me, these two would be without retirement accounts."

Hey, that was right. Merry had forgotten all about that. She wondered if April would allow her to withdraw some of that money for a new barrel-racing horse. That way, she could keep Tweety Pie. She was growing fond of the ornery S.O.B.

"That's a smart move," Dolly said. "So June..." Dolly whirled around to her, catching June with her mouth full. "Are you looking to take back the barrel-racing title from your sister next season?"

June chewed and swallowed. "No. I'm no longer competing. I've taken a job at Trent Campbell's rodeo school, teaching barrel racing."

Merry did a double take. She knew that had been June's part-time gig, but she figured going full-time was a few years off yet. Sure, June had said she wanted to retire from the rodeo, but Merry hadn't believed it.

"Did a certain assistant foreman at the Three Sisters Ranch factor into that decision?" Dolly asked.

"Yeah, I think Esteban and I might settle down and start a family."

Merry was glad she hadn't been drinking because that

would have had her choking. "A family?" Merry managed to get out.

"Eventually." June frowned at her.

"You're also attached to the Three Sisters Ranch, April, aren't you?"

"Yes. I'm getting married to Cole Lockwood. He's also a trainer at Trent's school."

"Congratulations. So, Merry…" Dolly turned her laser focus on to her. "Tell us about your significant other."

"I don't have one," she said. "I'm single and loving it. I hate to be tied down. In fact, right after Christmas, I'm jetting out to somewhere warm."

"You are?" June asked.

"Where are you going?" Dolly asked.

Merry blurted out the first thing that came to mind. "Tahiti."

"Are there rodeos in Tahiti?" Dolly asked.

"I don't know and I don't care. I'm going to sit my butt in the sand until the season starts." She wasn't quite sure how she was going to manage that, but maybe Carly and Zane would come through for her.

"When are you leaving?" Dolly asked.

"Right after the Jameson's charity ball. June and I were recipients of the rodeo scholarship many years ago, and we've been asked to give a short speech."

"Are you nervous?" Dolly asked.

"Just worried I'm going to drop an F-bomb in mixed company," Merry quipped.

"But you'll be back in time for the new rodeo season?"

"That's the plan," she said.

"Have you purchased a new barrel-racing horse yet?"

It was hard to keep the smile on her face, but Merry managed it. "Raphael is hard to replace."

"Yes, he will be."

Dolly continued to ask questions of all three of them. Merry could feel her sisters' curiosity like ants on her skin. This was the first they'd heard of her leaving Last Stand. Hell, she hadn't known it herself, until she had blurted it out.

There was no way her birthday and Christmas weren't going to suck this year if she stayed in Texas. And Luke had better not show up on her birthday.

Besides, Christmas without being with Simon in the cabin would be agony. No, she needed to get away. Merry was relieved when the interview was over and it was time to leave. She needed more whiskey than it would have been polite to ask for.

"Merry, one second," Dolly said.

"Yeah?"

"I noticed that you've got a really strong voice. Have you ever thought about starting your own podcast?"

"No. I wouldn't know where to begin." Merry wasn't good with new technology. She'd given up her flip phone, kicking and screaming. Although, she'd never go back. She was addicted to her smartphone now.

"If you're interested, I could show you the basics. I bet your fans would love to hear from you as you travel from rodeo to rodeo." Dolly leaned in conspiratorially. "And the ad money you get pays for gas and food."

"I'm in," Merry said.

"Stop on by after the holidays before you head out to Tahiti. I'm so jealous. I always wanted to go there."

"Yeah," Merry said with a small smile. "Me too."

"Maybe you can do your first podcast from the beach. As long as there's cell reception."

"I'll think about it." She didn't like keeping up the lie, so she wished Dolly a good day and hurried out of the Winnebago.

June and April were leaning up against her truck waiting for her.

"What's this single nonsense?" June asked.

"You just said that because you didn't want Dolly to ask about Simon's past, right?" April asked.

"I was going to tell you, but Simon and I broke up." It was hard to say.

"What happened?" April rubbed her shoulder in sympathy.

"He broke up with me," Merry said shortly.

"What did you do?" June asked.

"June!" April said, exasperated. "Merry, there has to be a mistake. Simon is crazy about you. Whatever happened, you can work it out."

"I don't think so." She explained the situation with Joyce and the letter.

"So you stole his letter?" June said.

"I didn't steal it."

"Does it belong to you?"

"Of course not."

"Did he ask for you to give it back to him?"

"Yes, but that's not the point," Merry said defensively.

"And you still have it."

"Of course I still have it. He would have destroyed it if I'd given it back to him."

"Merry, it's not your letter or your decision," June said. "No wonder he's pissed. Apologize and give him his letter back."

"He said some awful things to me," Merry said.

"I'm sure he's regretting saying them," April said. "But June's right. You had no business taking that letter." April held up her hands to stop Merry's rebuttal. "I know you acted from your heart, and that's why it hurt so much when he rejected your offer to help."

"He rejected me," Merry said, aghast that her voice cracked. "He tossed me to the curb after our first fight. It's over."

"Maybe it is, and maybe it isn't," April said. "But you need to give him his letter back."

"And don't open it and read it first," June said. "You won't be able to resist telling him what it said."

"Besides, it's none of your business," April added.

She hated that her sisters were right. "Fine. I'll give him back the stupid letter."

"And apologize," April said.

"Don't push it," Merry said between her teeth.

"Fine. Now, what's this about Tahiti?"

Merry looked at the toes of her boots. "You know that

retirement fund you have set up for me?"

"Absolutely not. You're not touching it."

"But I need to buy a barrel-racing horse."

"Why?" April put her hands on her hips. "It's not the barrel-racing title you want. It's the bronc-busting belt. You don't need a new horse for that."

"Besides," June said. "You don't have the time between now and February to buy a horse and get comfortable with it."

"Don't tell me what I can or can't do," Merry said.

"I wouldn't dream of it," June said, shaking her head. "I've got to get back to work. You might want to start looking for a pick-up job to make ends meet until the tournament."

"Pick-up job." Maybe she could be a pick-up rider when she wasn't competing. She wasn't sure if the WPRC allowed contestants to work at the events they were competing at. But she'd look into it. Hell, there was always bull fighting. She repressed a shudder. Or she could get a nice safe job somewhere. Looking back at the Winnebago, Merry wondered if this podcast idea had wings.

After her sisters left, Merry got into her truck and went for a drive. Main Street was opened up and the drive through the streets cheered her up a bit when she saw the wreaths on the lampposts and the decorations.

She pulled into the library parking lot and checked the balances on her credit cards. She had enough to get to San Antonio in February for the season's opening if she was frugal. If she sold Tweety Pie, she could buy a horse and compete in the all-around. But June had a point. Even if a horse appeared in their corral on Christmas morning, it would have had to be one of Santa's horses to get it up to speed by February.

"I'm willing to try it, if you are," she said to the universe.

She'd have to be content with staying on the bronc for eight seconds with more style and with a more challenging horse than LeAnn's.

Her thoughts kept going back to Simon. She had been out of line. Merry could admit that. But he immediately went to dumping her instead of trying to work it out. That wasn't what she needed in her life. Taking out her phone, she thumbed through her messages. He hadn't texted or called either.

Sure, it had only been a few days and she knew he was busy, but he still could have contacted her if he'd wanted to. She could take a hint. Unfortunately, she loved the jerk. She wished she didn't because getting over being dumped really sucked when your heart was involved.

Dejected, she wondered what she could do to cheer up. She hadn't heard from Carly and Zane since they left her in Argentina. Maybe they would be open to partying in Tahiti for New Year's Eve.

She texted them. Saw the three little dots and got excited. But then they disappeared and no message came through. So much for Tahiti.

Chapter Nineteen

S IMON LOOKED AROUND the Jameson House and was quietly impressed. It was a beautiful Victorian farmhouse decorated with a style and class that Braxton Reynolds had never managed to achieve, but secretly longed for.

And there he was thinking about the old man again, instead of enjoying the free booze and the soothing sounds of a three-piece jazz band. The ball was to benefit a scholarship given to a promising teenager to use for rodeoing. He had suspected that Merry and June had been recipients, but he'd had his thoughts confirmed when he saw their pictures up on the wall of past beneficiaries. They were going to be here tonight.

The thought of seeing Merry again filled him with equal parts dread and desire.

"You bunch clean up nice," Charlie said. In his hand was probably not his first glass of wine.

"We try."

"Have you given any thought of what comes next for you?" Charlie asked.

"No, I'm taking it day by day," Simon said.

His gaze snagged on June Grayson, who was wearing a

pearl-colored crystal dress that barely covered her ass. Esteban had his hands full glaring down the would-be Romeos whose eyes caught the glittery fire when those crystals hit the candlelight.

"Is there anything I can do?" Charlie asked.

"No, but thanks."

They both watched Emily Sullivan and her husband Donovan waltz around the ballroom.

"I wanted to say that I admire how you don't try and force yourself into his life," Simon said.

"I'm subtle about it, but I'm here for him in case he ever wants to talk to me—or shout at me."

"Or ignore the fact that you exist?"

"That too. But it doesn't change the fact that I'm here, does it?" Charlie took a long pull on his wine.

"If he doesn't want a reconciliation, would you ever write him a letter to be handed to him after you died?"

"That's a very specific question," Charlie said.

When Simon didn't respond, Charlie thought about it. "It hadn't occurred to me. I suppose I could spill my guts out. But that doesn't seem very fair. Donny wouldn't be able to respond to what I was saying. And after I'm gone, what would be the point? At best, he'd forgive me and then spend the rest of his life regretting that he hadn't reconciled with me while I was alive. At worst, he'd be bitter and pissed off because he couldn't tell me to go to hell before I got there."

"Yeah." Simon nodded. "That's how I see it too. Thanks."

"I'm not sure for what. Uh-oh, here comes trouble."

Simon had already seen her. If June's dress had caused a commotion, Merry's was sending men into cardiac arrest. She was wearing a scrap of red fabric that Simon supposed could be called a dress. Her blond hair was plaited down her back in a tight braid that called attention to her high cheekbones and bright blue eyes.

"Son, if I were thirty years younger, I'd hit you over the head with a shovel if you were standing in my way of her."

"I'm not in anyone's way. Not anymore," he said.

"Then why is she coming this way?"

Simon wasn't sure, but he liked the view. And sure enough, she stopped in front of them. "Can I talk to you in private?"

"Excuse me," Charlie said, and faded into the distance.

Reaching into her purse, Merry came up with the letter and thrust it at him. "Here. I'm sorry."

She turned to leave.

Stunned, he let the packet fall to the ground. He caught her by the elbow and when she whirled around on him, he let her go and stepped back. "Wait," he said.

"What?" she snapped out.

"I'm sorry, too."

Looking away, she shrugged. "I was a bitch. I get it. Anyway, see you around."

"Merry, wait," he said.

"Why?"

He caught a few people's eyes as he searched around for a private corner. "People are starting to stare. Let's find a quiet place to talk."

"I said what I came here to say," she said.

"Please?"

"Fine," she huffed out.

There wasn't a private space in the entire house, so he guided her outside and into his car. She shook her arm free.

"I'm not going anywhere with you. I have to give a speech in a few minutes."

"Let's just sit and talk where no one can overhear us."

"Do we have to do this now?"

"No," he said. "You can come home with me later and we can talk at the cabin."

Shaking her head, Merry crossed her arms over her chest. "You've got five minutes."

"I'll take it," he said under his breath and opened the door to the car for her. He tried not to get distracted by her long legs or the way the dress clung to her curves. What the hell had he been thinking, letting her walk away from him?

Once he was inside the car with her, the memories flooded over him. She was such a part of his life and always would be. He needed her to know that. And if she still wanted him to fuck off, then he would. "I overreacted," he said.

"You think?" She wasn't going to give him an inch, and he didn't deserve it.

"I shouldn't have said the things I did. I was exhausted and at the end of my rope about a lot of things. I took out my frustration on you."

"If you meant what you said, have the balls to stand behind them."

"That's the whole point. I didn't mean them. Seeing that letter really fucked me up. It was the third letter he'd sent to me."

"He sent two others?" Merry cocked her head at him.

"Yeah, and I destroyed the other two, but they keep on coming. I've been trying so hard to put him behind me that I pushed you away too. I never meant to do that."

"It sounded like you did. You immediately went to ending things instead of waiting until we cooled down. That really hurt." She turned to face him for the first time.

"I'm sorry. I didn't mean what I said. I lashed out in anger. I don't want to break up with you. You're the best thing in my life right now. I might not know where I'm going to be next month, but I always thought I'd still have you."

"You have a funny way of showing it," she grumbled, but unless he was imagining it, her posture was less stiff than before.

"Can we pretend that the other night didn't happen?"

"I can't do that," she said. "Because it did."

Simon nodded. He supposed that would have been too much to hope for. "I'm thinking of taking a ranch position in Houston next year. There's a cattle ranch out there that's looking for hands until after the spring calving."

"Houston? That's a ways away," she said softly.

"Yeah, I figure I can put the house up on the market and hopefully it will sell while I'm gone."

"Good luck," she said. "I should be getting back."

When she would have left the car, he placed a gentle hand on her shoulder. "I still have a few minutes left from the five you gave me."

"Simon." Her head lolled back on the headrest. "What's the point? You're leaving anyway."

"The point is I love you."

She gaped at him.

"Holy shit, I shocked you into silence."

"Bite me," Merry said, recovering. "You love me? You have a hell of a way of showing it."

"I was pissed off."

"Are you going to break up with me every time you get pissed off at me? Because if that's how it's going to be, we might as well stay apart."

"No," he said. "Never again. I promise."

She looked out the window and he'd have given anything to know what she was thinking. Luckily, he soon found out.

"Seeing Luke and his two kids really fucked with my head. You were right that I was projecting some of my emotions on that letter."

"It's okay. I understand."

"So where does that leave us?"

Hope flickered in his chest. "So you forgive me?"

"I'm not sure yet. But I think so."

"Merry, I'm a hot mess right now. I've got nothing to offer you that's mine. I don't want anything tainted by my father to touch us again, but I'm still working through a lot of things."

"I know," she said, holding his hand. "You've been through so much these past ten years and you've only been out of prison a few weeks. I should have cut you some slack. I should have given you the envelope back sooner. Speaking of which, where the hell is it?"

Simon patted his jacket. "Shit, I think I dropped it in the house."

"Well, we better go find it." Merry made to leave again

and again he stopped her.

"It's not important. It never was." He cupped her cheek in his hand. Closing his eyes, he kissed her soft mouth. She tasted like champagne and strawberries and when her arms came around his neck, he was home. The smell of the leather seats, the feel of her soft body pressing against him, was all he wanted in the world.

Simon could have spent all night kissing her, but her phone began to ring.

"Oh hell, who has us up on Instagram now?" she muttered. "What?" she snarled into the phone. "Oh shit!" She hung up. "I've got to go. My speech is next."

He watched her hurry back inside. He needed a few minutes to compose himself. He could have lost her for good because of his father. He would never let that happen again. He was going to find that letter and let her open it up and read it. If she wanted to tell him what it said, fine. If not, that was fine too. But at least she wouldn't have to worry about him regretting never reading the letter.

Simon walked in on the tail end of Merry's speech. He clapped politely with everyone else, but he was distracted in trying to find the envelope. It wasn't on the floor where they had been standing. And none of the catering staff remembered seeing it.

"Sometimes the trash takes itself out," he murmured and went to find two glasses of champagne, one for him and one for his lady.

Chapter Twenty

NOW THAT THE cabin was ready to be decorated for Christmas, they had to find the perfect tree. Merry wasn't sure how she and Simon were going to work everything out, but she was willing to wait and see. Especially, if it meant that she could spend her birthday and Christmas with him. It was better than Tahiti.

"Did you have a type of tree in mind?" Simon asked once they got to the tree farm.

"A big one," she said.

Simon got out his phone. "It says here that the most common one to get is the Virginia pine. Do you want to get it flocked?"

"That sounds dirty. What is it?"

"It's when they paint the branches white so it looks like it snowed." He pointed to one that was pre-cut and resting in a bucket of water.

"That is pretty, but it looks fake. I'd rather have a plain green one and add some tinsel to it to make it sparkle."

"You're the boss."

Merry went down the rows of trees. The pine smell was sweet and she remembered a time when her father was with them for Christmas. Luke had had it in his head to make wreaths to sell, and they all pitched in as a family to put the pine branches on the wire frame. It had been her mother's job to tie the ribbons on them, while Merry and her sisters sorted the branches for Luke. She remembered how sticky her hands had become from the tree sap, and how the smell lingered in the barn and inside the trailer for days.

"What are you thinking about?" Simon asked.

"My father Luke loved the pine trees, but we only had artificial trees."

"Why?"

"He thought it was a waste of money. I wonder if his new family had a real tree," she said.

"Don't be sad," he said.

"I'm not. Not anymore. It was just one more thing I need to let go of. He wasn't a great father," Merry said. "My mother stepped up a lot to make up for the fact that we didn't have our fathers in our lives. I know things have been pretty hostile between the two of you, but I'd like to reach out to her again and see if she'll join us on Christmas Day."

"Of course," he said.

"Thanks." She hugged him.

In the end, she picked out a six-foot tree. It was smaller than she had wanted, but her ankle wouldn't let her carry any more than that.

"Why this one instead of the bigger one?" he asked.

"We're going to have a hard enough time wrestling this through the door."

"Get the tree you want. I'll ask the guys at the ranch to

help out."

"They'd do that?" Merry asked.

"For you, they'd do anything. You've got quite the following."

"Are you sure?"

"They aren't the only ones who would do anything for you," Simon said. "Pick the tree that sings to your heart."

Merry hugged him tight, blinking back tears. The words "*I love you*" almost slipped out of her mouth. She held on to him longer than normal, wondering if she meant that like, "*I love you for doing this for me*" or if she meant it like, "*I love you.*"

Holy crap that was some scary shit.

"You okay?" he asked.

"I'm great." She kissed him and then busied herself finding the perfect tree for her special Christmas.

A BUNCH OF the ranch hands and some of the retreat members said they would come over to the cabin after dinner to help take the tree off her truck and set it up in the living room. Simon helped her bake cookies and taste-tested the eggnog recipe. He wound up dozing on the new couch for most of the afternoon. She put a batch of chili in the Crock-Pot and called her mother for tips on how to season it so it was flavorful, and not just five-alarm hot.

"Add some cocoa," Penny said.

"Are you trying to sabotage my chili?" Merry scowled.

"Trust me. Just make sure it's unsweetened cocoa."

"All right," she said skeptically. "Are you done wrapping all those presents from the giving tree or do you need help?"

"We're done. How's the tree coming along?"

"It's still on my truck. The ranch hands are going to come and help us set it up."

"He's really well liked at the Three Sisters Ranch, isn't he?" Penny asked.

"Yeah, I keep telling you he's a good guy."

"Esteban seems to like him. Cole, too."

"There's something you should know," Merry said. "It might piss you off."

"What now?" Penny groaned.

Merry paused and looked over at him snoring on the couch. "I love him, Mama."

"Oh hell," her mother said.

"Thanks."

"I was afraid of that."

"There's nothing to be afraid of," Merry said. "It is what it is."

"You never did do things the easy way."

"This kind of feels easy," she said with a smile.

"Have you told him yet?"

"I just figured it out myself."

"Look," her mother said. "I still don't completely trust Simon."

Merry closed her eyes. She didn't want to get into this right now.

"But that's only going to come with time and exposure.

So I guess what I'm saying is, if we're still invited, I'd like to move our Christmas celebration over to the cabin."

"What?" Merry's eyes flew open. She was certain she heard that wrong.

"Well, are we still invited or what?"

"Of course," Merry said. "Of course you are."

"I need access to his kitchen on your birthday to make the lasagna."

Merry nibbled on her lower lip. That would cut into sexy times a bit, but she was sure her mother would want to leave before it got dark. "No problem," she said, hoping that it wouldn't be.

"We'll see about that. But I'm prepared to do my part," her mother said grumpily. "And I'll apologize to him for being a righteous bitch."

Merry snorted. "I'm sure he'll accept it."

"And I'll try to do better," Penny grumbled.

"It's going to be the best Christmas ever," Merry said, unable to stop the giddy feeling bubbling up inside of her.

"If we're all together, then it will be."

Just in case, though, Merry decided to double down and bake a few more batches of Christmas cookies. While she had her mother on the line, she got those recipes too.

MERRY WASN'T SURE she was being smart about Simon, but it didn't matter. She loved the idiot and intended to tell him that tonight. It was her birthday, and they were planning on a special dinner after her mother left the house. Right now, Penny was in Simon's kitchen preparing her famous lasagna. June and April had also stopped by to bring platters of food. April stayed behind to help their mother, but June and Merry had to head over to the fire station to help hand out presents.

"Do you think we have enough food?" June asked, tugging on her elf costume in the truck.

Merry was already dressed. The stockings were candy-cane-striped but they were a size too small and were cutting off her circulation. She was considering peeling them off and going bare-legged.

"Mama is cooking enough lasagna to feed all of Last Stand. You made a beef brisket. April made a ham. I've baked every pie you could think of. I don't think anyone is going to go hungry."

Simon had decided to have a Christmas open house for anyone who wanted to spend the day with them. A few of the ranch hands said they'd stop by in the afternoon. And she was looking forward to playing Christmas records and dancing around the living room. And once everyone left, she was looking forward to some alone time with the man she loved.

"Are you ready to do this?" Merry asked as they parked outside of the fire station.

"Ho, ho, ho."

"Who are you callin' a ho?" she joked.

They spent a couple of hours handing out toys and presents to the children who needed them. Simon and his retreat group were there also, serving popcorn and hot chocolate. While the kids watched a Christmas cartoon, Merry snuck up next to Simon.

"Come with me," she breathed in his ear.

Reaching for his hand, she led him out of the room and deeper into the fire station.

"Where are you taking me, you wicked elf?"

"I was hoping for an excuse to take these stockings off," she said, leading him into the equipment room.

"Are you sure you want to do this here?" he asked.

"It's just a little quickie," she said, sinking to her knees in front of him.

"Oh, Merry," he moaned as she unbuttoned his pants and reached into his underwear to pull his cock out.

"Now here's a candy cane I want to lick." She traced her tongue up and down his cock.

Simon's eyes grew hooded and his fingers tangled in her hair. When she took him deep into her throat, he groaned and rocked slowly against her. "That feels amazing," he said.

Bobbing her head in a fast rhythm, she enjoyed the feel of him sliding in and out of her mouth. She rubbed the shaft while she hollowed out her cheeks to suck him hard. Cupping his balls, she licked over the tip of him.

Simon went up on his toes and his entire body tensed. "I'm going to come," he gritted out.

She increased her efforts, loving the power she had over him in that moment. When he came, he shuddered and his knees wobbled. Swallowing, she laughed and stood up.

"Merry Christmas," she said, kissing him.

"Where do you think you're going?" he asked, when she would have walked away. "I believe you said you wanted out of these stockings."

Running his hands under her little skirt, he rolled the tight fabric of her stockings down over her hips, taking her underpants with him. He stepped on them so she could pull her feet out.

"I'm going to need my panties," she said and went to reach for them.

"Not just yet," he breathed and kissed her slowly while his fingers pushed inside her.

He fingered her fast and she loved the thrilling caress. It felt like they were just getting started and she reveled in how he knew just how to touch her.

"I love you," she gasped when his flickering movements pushed her over the edge into an orgasm that curled her toes.

"What did you say?" Simon was shocked, but he didn't stop playing with her.

"Shit," she said. "I was saving that for later."

"Do you mean it?" he asked.

"Yes, yes, yes." Her eyes closed as she danced into another orgasm, quick on the heels of the other.

"I like the sound of that." He spun her around so she was facing the wall. Spreading her legs wide, he pushed up her skirt. "It's a good thing I came prepared."

She looked over her shoulder to see him opening a packet with his teeth and then rolling a condom over his hard length. Sliding his cock inside her, Simon grunted in pleasure. Pushing back against him, she pressed her lips together to keep from screaming out how good he felt when he thrust his entire length inside her. He fucked her hard and fast, barely giving her time to recover from the two quick orgasms.

She could hear the Christmas carols starting and she choked off a laugh. "There's no way we're getting on Santa's nice list after this."

"Ask me if I care?" Simon said, his voice shaking and filled with need.

It set off another set of tingles throughout her body. And when he finished with several hard thrusts, she clamped down around him and rode out yet another dizzying orgasm.

"Oh crap, I can't walk straight," she said as he yanked down her skirt and fixed her clothes. Then he disposed of the condom and zipped himself up.

He kissed her until they both settled. "I love you too," he said. "Just remember you're not wearing underwear when you sit down."

"Yeah, that's not happening." Merry hastily retrieved her stockings and slid on her underwear. Stuffing the stockings into the nearest trash can, she held hands with Simon as they walked back to the venue.

"Happy birthday, baby," Simon said.

"Merry Christmas, cowboy," she said with a wink.

><

MERRY WAS STILL in bed wrapped around Simon when her family rang the doorbell Christmas morning. She made them wait while she pulled on her red plaid pajamas. Simon followed down shortly afterward and once the coffee was made and the cinnamon buns were consumed, they all convened in the living room.

June hooked up her iPhone so she could get her Christmas playlist going. In addition to the classics, there were some songs from the eighties and nineties that had them laughing and singing along while they opened up their presents.

Their mother loved the Coach purse they had all gone in on to buy her.

April loved the jewelry that Merry and June had picked out. "I'm going to wear the earrings and the necklace on my wedding day," she said.

"That's what we had in mind," Merry said.

The guys got cologne and sensible things like new work gloves and sturdy insulated mugs that could keep coffee warm or iced tea cold. Their mother gave each of them gift cards and some cash.

"Thanks, Mama," Merry said, holding up the gas card. "This is going to come in handy."

"Here," June said, thrusting a small box at her. "This will come in handy too."

Merry had given June the turquoise necklace that she had been eyeballing when they went shopping for April's jewelry. Merry opened the box and took out a horse ornament.

"It looks just like Athena. You couldn't find one that looked like Raphael?" Merry joked.

"Well, there's a deeper meaning in that ornament," June said. "I'm not going to need Athena this year since I'm not competing. I want you to have her for the season."

Merry almost dropped the ornament. "What?"

"Look, I know she'll never replace Raphael. But she's worked with you before and she knows how we ride. She'll give you the advantage that a new horse couldn't give you. And you'll have a fighting chance of winning the all-around with her."

Merry was trying to hold back her tears, but they flooded her eyes anyway.

"Oh stop blubbering," June said, coming over to hug her.

"I don't know what to say," Merry babbled.

"Thank you is a good start."

"Thank you." She squeezed June tight.

"Go kick some ass."

Merry was still reeling from that when Simon handed her his gift.

"What's this?" she asked, feeling the slim package.

"Open it and find out."

Merry carefully slid her finger under the tape and un-wrapped the shiny paper carefully.

"Oh, just rip it open already," April said. "I'm dying to see what it is."

It was an envelope. But it was too thin to be his father's letter. She looked at him quizzically as she opened the letter. It was a printed airline ticket.

"To Tahiti?" she screamed.

"We'll be in Tahiti for New Year's Eve," he said. "I booked us on a two-week vacation in one of those huts in the middle of the water."

"I can't believe you," she said.

"We're going to have a busy schedule next year and we won't be seeing a lot of each other. I want to start the year off with some memories that will sustain us while I'm in Houston and you're on the circuit."

She kissed him.

"Okay that's enough," her mother said. "We don't need a demonstration of those memories. Keep it clean for my sake, will you?"

They ignored her and kept kissing.

Merry was pretty sure that next year was going to be the best year ever. She had her family, an experienced barrel-racing horse to end her rodeo career with, and of course, Simon Reynolds, her high school sweetheart who'd always been the man of her dreams. He was her Christmas miracle.

Epilogue

One year later

MERRY WAS BACK home in Last Stand. The rodeo season was over and she and Athena were officially retired. Raphael was happy to have them both back. Simon's father's house had sold quickly and Simon had set up a foundation in his mother's name that gave out grants for alcoholics who needed money for treatments. She and Simon were living together in the cabin, although they'd expanded it a little, adding a garage for his Corvette and a barn for Tweety Pie, Raphael and Pixie.

Pixie was the horse she was planning on using when she was a pick-up rider during the bronc-busting and bull-riding events. The pick-up riders and bullfighters had always had her back—now it was her turn to make sure the riders stayed safe. When she wasn't doing that, though, she was growing her podcast and waiting for an announcer's job to free up.

"Hello, future Mrs. Reynolds," Simon said, coming up behind her and wrapping his arms around her. He had proposed last night on her birthday, but she had known it was coming.

"You're up early," she said, leaning back into him.

The last year had been hard on them both. They had tried to talk or text daily, but they'd both found it difficult being apart for so long. They'd had fights and made up, long distance. Whenever they could, they had stolen a night here and there to be together, but that had been bittersweet because all too soon, they'd had to go their separate ways again. But that was all over now. Simon's Houston contract had ended. They had kept him well past spring calving and he was set to start at the Three Sisters Ranch as a hand in January.

"I wanted to make sure your family didn't get us out of bed this year," Simon said.

"I don't know. I kind of liked that tradition."

"Well, then let's go back to bed." He started to drag her backward.

"They're here," she said.

"Later for you," Simon vowed, and stood next to her as they welcomed her mother and her new boyfriend, Charlie Lincoln.

She hoped the silver fox didn't break her mother's heart. But they seemed to get along very well.

June and Esteban were next, followed by April and Cole.

As usual, they had cooked for an army and hopefully some of the ranch hands would be joining them later, the way they had last year. After devouring the breakfast casserole she had made, they all tromped to the living room to open presents.

This was the perfect Christmas, Merry decided. She was in her own home, with her fiancé and her family around her.

The Christmas tree was decorated with their own ornaments and she would enjoy building on the Christmas memories for years to come.

"I've got something for you," Charlie said to Simon. "It's not really a Christmas present though."

He handed him a thick envelope.

It took Merry a minute to recognize that it was the same package from Simon's father that she had taken from him last year, and he had subsequently lost.

"I picked it up when you dropped it. I wanted to keep it until you were back in Last Stand for good, or you had settled somewhere else."

"Thank you," Simon said. He held it out to Merry. "I want you to have it."

"Do you want me to read it?" she asked.

"You can do whatever you want with it. I don't care. I'll never ask you what it says and I never want to know. But I almost lost you once by not letting you keep that letter. I'm not going to make the same mistake twice."

"Are you sure?" Merry asked.

"He has no more power over me."

She nodded. She tapped the letter against her hand, thinking about how much pain and suffering a father could give their child. And how much redemption they could bring with a simple apology. This packet didn't seem like an apology. She flicked it into the fire.

"Merry," her mother gasped.

"It's okay," she said. "It was nothing."

She reached out and held Simon's hand. He was smiling

broadly at her. "I love you," he said.

"I love you too."

And just like that, Merry had the Christmas she'd always wanted. Especially since she had one more surprise for Simon. Her hand drifted down to her belly. But that one she could keep until they were alone tonight.

As they went to open their presents, she ran her finger over the all-around trophy that she won this year and the belt buckle that had her name on it with a bucking bronco on it—Merry Grayson, the first champion rider in the bronc-busting category.

"Sorry, LeAnn," she murmured. But she wasn't really.

The End

Want more? Check out June and Esteban's story in
A Cowboy for June!

Join Tule Publishing's newsletter for more great reads and weekly deals!

If you enjoyed *A Cowboy for Merry*,
you'll love the other books in the…

Three Sisters Ranch series

Book 1: *The Cowboy's Daughter*

Book 2: *The Cowboy's Hunt*

Book 3: *The Cowboy's Heart*

Book 4: *A Cowboy for April*

Book 5: *A Cowboy for June*

Book 6: *A Cowboy for Merry*

Available now at your favorite online retailer!

About the Author

USA Today bestselling author, Jamie K. Schmidt, writes erotic contemporary love stories and paranormal romances. Her steamy, romantic comedy, Life's a Beach, reached #65 on USA Today, #2 on Barnes & Noble and #9 on Amazon and iBooks. Her Club Inferno series from Random House's Loveswept line has hit both the Amazon and Barnes & Noble top one hundred lists. The first book in the series, Heat, put her on the USA Today bestseller list for the first time, and is a #1 Amazon bestseller. Her book Stud is a 2018 Romance Writers of America Rita® Finalist in Erotica. Her dragon paranormal romance series has been called "fun and quirky" and "endearing." Partnered with New York Times bestselling author and former porn actress, Jenna Jameson, Jamie's hardcover debut, SPICE, continues Jenna's FATE trilogy.

Thank you for reading

A Cowboy for Merry

If you enjoyed this book, you can find more from all our great authors at TulePublishing.com, or from your favorite online retailer.

TULE
PUBLISHING

Printed in Great Britain
by Amazon